MW01016426

Chronicles of Ha Ha Bay

(Be true to your roots)

Chronicles of Ha Ha Bay

A COLLECTION OF STORIES

Edward Bessey

Illustrated by: Gil Balbuena Jr.

Copyright © 2011 by Edward Bessey.

Library of Congress Control Number: 2011903139

ISBN:	Hardcover	978-1-4568-7691-3
	Softcover	978-1-4568-7690-6
	Ebook	978-1-4568-7692-0

All rights reserved. No part of this book may be reproduced or transmitted in any form or by any means, electronic or mechanical, including photocopying, recording, or by any information storage and retrieval system, without permission in writing from the copyright owner.

NOTE:
This is a work of fiction. However, most chronicles are based on actual events, often dramatized and/or sensationalized to underscore tragic, and sometimes hilarious, events in Newfoundland's forgotten history. Any direct resemblances to actual people or places, unless specifically indicated, to those portrayed in this novel are purely coincidental.

This book was printed in the United States of America.

To order additional copies of this book, contact:
Xlibris Corporation
1-888-795-4274
www.Xlibris.com
Orders@Xlibris.com
93872

Contents

Prologue

Ha Ha Bay

The land God gave to Cain.

From his own log, Jacques Cartier, in late May 1534, stopped with two ships in a sheltered bay within a bay on his voyage to New France. He named it St. Anthony's Haven. But local folklore has it that soon after leaving, he sailed around the northern tip of Giovanni Caboto's Terra Nova (Newfoundland) and became stranded in the ice floes in the narrow Detroit de Belle Isle (Strait of Belle Isle) between Terra Nova and Terra Lavrador (Labrador) and was driven toward land in a storm toward a small isle about three miles long and about three hundred feet high.

Delighted to find open water in a small channel between the isle and the mainland, he decided to search for a small cove and heave to until the pack ice moved offshore, explore the isle, find a suitable rock to behead a few rebellious sailors, and erect a banner to duly claim it for the glory of France.

It was in a typical North Atlantic nor 'easterly gale that he attempted to sail around the isle from the easterly side, only to find his passage blocked by what looked, through his spyglass, like a tall picketed fence. After moving closer for inspection, it was revealed that the isle actually had trees with a long barren cape and was connected to the mainland by a low isthmus that was covered in very tall grasses, making it appear as a fenced barrier, or *haha,* as he logged it.

In his panic to tack away, he launched four boats with rowers to help prevent his two ships from being blown ashore on the haha but lost two of his rowboats on the huge breakers.

Some hours later, after great difficulty and to the relief of all, he managed to sail around the cape and anchor on the leeward side of the haha. He landed and explored the little isle to find the outer cape was covered with giant limestone slabs with myriads of unique flowers and lichens in between.

He stayed in the small sheltered cove beyond the haha for some two weeks, took on food and water, and carried out his chores—a few lashings and a beheading. As per standard protocol, their daily evening cook-ups were held on the seashore whenever possible to break the monotony of long ship voyages. One day, a high wind picked up and the fire spread, burning all the trees on the little peninsula. He thus named it Ile Brule (Burnt Island). The cape had some unique flowers that he believed grew only in the subtropics, so he collected a few specimens of plants to take back for observation.

Next day on June 7, the strait became passable, and Cartier quickly squared his yards and sailed off toward Labrador, sorely disappointed but greatly relieved.

Cartier considered such a treacherous and inhospitable land unsuitable to claim for a great king like Francis I, who had sponsored his voyage, and justified its rejection in his log by describing it as "a godforsaken land, the likes of which God would give to Cain." He named the treacherous bay Baie Haha (Ha Ha Bay).

Word soon reached King Henry VIII through Basque whalers, who had frequented the bay for years searching for humpbacks and rights, that Jacques Cartier had taken procession of a beautiful flower-covered subtropical isle in England's New Founde Lande for France and christened it Ha Ha Bay as a joke then burned it to humiliate him.

The snub so infuriated Henry VIII, who was also claiming to be the rightful king of France, that he quickly mobilized three top-of-the-line ships, his most powerful man-o'-wars, to reclaim his precious possession and restore his dignity.

Upon arriving in Ha Ha Bay, the warships soon located the large bloodstained rock with an old worn-out cat-o'-nine-tails nearby and the two wrecked rowboats on the isthmus, attesting to the authenticity of the Basque's story, and therefore sailed off after Jacques Cartier in hot pursuit.

Intercepting the French expedition near Stadacone, New France, the British soon learned from Cartier's log that the he had actually named it *the Land God Gave to Cain* and that *haha* was his old French spelling for the dangerous narrow strip of land connecting the isle to the mainland—in short, an obstruction or dead end. Furthermore, the ship's botanist revealed the flowers were actually of the high arctic variety. Red-faced, the English released the two French ships.

Be that legend, myth, or fact, the bay is still called Ha Ha Bay to this day—the community has been renamed Raleigh in honor of the British battleship HMS *Raleigh* that was lost at Point Armour, Labrador, fifteen miles away—and has a Frenchman's Rock on the leeward side of the cape with blood stains. The local tars and fishermen still spin yarns of seeing two full-rigged French frigates sail into the bay and head directly toward the haha—now Old Man's Neck—whenever there's a nor'easter brewing; and on a calm night, if you have the stamina to hike up over the Burnt Cape to Cannon Holes or Big Oven after midnight and listen, you can still hear Francis I laughing.

The little peninsula is now known internationally as Burnt Cape Ecological Reserve, boasting thirty-four kinds of our planet's rarest lichens and flowers, with one species being found nowhere else in the world; but officially, all marine charts still use Cartier's version—Burnt Island.

Chronicle 1

The Newfoundland Hurricane

They that go down to the sea in ships do business in great waters.

Few stories throughout Newfoundland's turbulent seafaring history are as tragic, or as obscure, as the Newfoundland Hurricane that occurred in the late summer of 1775. While local historians may rightly overpublicize and overdramatize such horrific loss of life as caused by the sinking of the *Titanic*, World War I, World War II, the Halifax Explosion, or the *Greenland* sealing disaster, they pale compared to the Newfoundland Hurricane.

For two days in the autumn of 1775, it had been an eerily flat calm on the Grand Banks as fishing schooners, fully laden to the gunnels with cod, lay waiting for wind to commence their homeward voyage when, unknown to them, the Independence Hurricane that had ravaged the coastal United States before moving offshore suddenly veered toward Newfoundland. At the same time, a deep Arctic depression was moving south from the Labrador and was stalled over Avalon Peninsula. Without warning, just past midnight on September 9, the Arctic depression collided with the Category 5 hurricane, and within forty-eight hours, over one hundred fishing schooners were wrecked, including two Royal Navy patrol ships, countless inshore fishing boats, and nearly 4,200 people were dead. And one of these unfortunate captains was Richard Buckle, a distant relative of mine, who, with nearly every member of his family, were on an old fishing schooner built in Dublin with the unfortunate name *The Lucky Shamrock.*

As a nine-year-old, I recall sitting by an old potbelly stove with tears in my eyes, listening with mixed emotions to this epic tale being related to me by my aged grandfather that had been passed down to him by his foster father.

"If I could just turn back the pages of time, my boy," he usually began solemnly, as a prerequisite to his yarns, "I'd be a better man."

He never once explained why, but all his life believed he was a bad man and talked directly to children as if to compensate for some lost youth or regrets for some lesson he had learned too late. Then he would pause and indicate for me to pull my stool closer to the stove and get comfortable. I obeyed without a whimper. He often overused me as his sounding board, but nonetheless, I loved to listen and was proud to have him as a grandfather, even though back then, in his eighties, most of his friends had passed away, and many of his stories were about death.

"This is a true tale about a relative of yours, Captain Buckle. His parents were Normans, poor fisherfolk, born to peasants in Brittany. Life was bloody tough in those days, my boy, but they refused to knuckle down and be anyone's slaves. No, sir! Because of that, some Frenchy compte forced them to escape to England in a tiny punt, all ten of them, with nothing, not even food. A month later, barely alive, they reached Lancaster and settled there, the witch-burning town."

"Witches are real?" I whispered nervously.

"No. That's another story. Just listen."

He pensively filled his pipe with tobacco as he formulated his story, lit it with a burning chunk of wood from the stove, took a few passionate puffs, coughed a few times, and continued.

"Now theirs was a lesson in tragedy. Wasn't in England a year before they were all dead, except the youngest son, Richard, who was only twelve. Smallpox. Wasn't used to crowded, dirty places. The—"

"Is that like chicken pox?" I interrupted, cringing at the thoughts of my worst illness and my spotted, scabby body for months.

"Worse. You won't get it here. Too clean. And isolated."

Blowing smoke between his missing upper front teeth, he sighed deeply and returned to his tale.

"That town was cursed. Catholics said witches lived in the old castle there, that it was the fault of the protestant Queen Elizabeth I for beheading Mary. But young Richard was nobody's fool, he knew about politics and wouldn't get involved in them Wars of the Roses, so he crossed the Irish Sea and joined a fishing schooner out of Dublin that worked the western banks here in Newfoundland. With smarts forced upon him by terrible hardships and from fishing with his father in the North Sea, in four years, at only sixteen, he was first mate on *The Lucky Shamrock.*

"Richard was a big, burly young man. Yet handsome. A heathen that cursed at the drop of a hat, but still, for some unknown reason, the Good Lord intervened and gave him his blessing. He was fortunate enough to meet a good, hardworking Protestant woman, Ruth Fowler, who homesteaded during the winter near Carbonear, which was illegal at the time. She had lost her husband hunting seals off Notre Dame Bay, common in those days, and had three children to feed, all girls under sixteen. She was in St. John's looking for a captain to take over her husband's schooner and his fishing gear, who would in turn agree look after them. There she met the captain, Sean O'Riley, of *The Lucky Shamrock* at church service, who sought out Richard in a local pub and introduced them. Sorely disappointed, Ruth considered Richard too young, too inexperienced, too aggressive, far too headstrong, and worse, a heavy drinker, but with three starving daughters, she hadn't much choice and offered him the position. Richard readily agreed and opted to stay for the winter with them.

"During that first winter, Richard showed his leadership; he hired two strong, adventurous young men his own age from the area to help him in lieu of future payment. They fixed up Ruth's house, repaired the schooner, mended the fishing nets, and got her back on her feet. She was grateful and impressed, but Richard, in her words, was "like a wild savage, as bad as the Red Indians." So as he worked, she sat with him in the fishing sheds and taught him how to be civilized, read, mannerly around her daughters, and how to act godly. She soon recognized he was exceptionally smart, a born leader. All was easy, except trying to teach him religion; that was a lost cause. He despised it with a passion. It had been the demise of his family, and just mentioning it would set him off.

"Then in March, tragedy struck again; scarlet fever hit the town, and Ruth Fowler died slowly and painfully—choked to death. Richard, still only seventeen, was now left to look after her three children and their property. With his arrogance, the challenge was right up his alley."

After a brief interruption from Grandmother with a warning not to teach me any nonsense or smut, to which Grandfather flippantly nodded his head in compliance, the story resumed.

"What happened next is only hearsay, mind you. Women's gossip most likely, but they say the next winter after their mother died was bitterly cold, and they all slept together in one big bed for warmth. Nobody knows for sure, but one thing is certain, they all lived together and prospered, and within twenty years, they owned half the property in the bay. Respected by everybody, even visited by the colonial governor of Newfoundland, Robert Duff. It's also rumored that the girls all loved and cherished his rugged and aggressive mentality, even competing for his affection. Be that true or not, what is true is that he fathered eight children, five sons and three daughters, by those three beautiful, cultured young ladies, even though he'd be gone to sea for most of the year. Preachers say that's when the Good Lord took back his blessing.

"In the spring of 1774, his old shipmates drifted into Carbonear in *The Lucky Shamrock* with a tragic story. Leaking like a sieve, the ship was barely afloat, a total wreck. Its masts shot away, half its sailors dead, and scurvy raging aboard. A skeleton, everything worthwhile stolen. Their captain and mate dead. Nobody knew navigation. A pitiful sight. Reached Carbonear only by the grace of God. Got caught in the bloody Seven Years' War between France and England. A victim of those bloody, roaming, raiding parties from the American colonies, revolutionaries."

To me, back then, Grandfather's logic was confusing. Richard was at times good and sometimes bad. I didn't know where these countries were or the people involved but understood they were far away across the ocean and guessed Richard was going to end up a hero by saving them. Grandfather's stories were like that, first bad, then good. He liked heroes and happy endings, as did I, but he told his yarns exactly the way he had heard them, inserting his own commentary on the parts he deemed questionable.

"Which side are the revolutionaries on?" I queried excitedly, now hypnotized by his heightening passionate deliverance and trying to determine who destroyed their ship, hoping they were pirates; they always fascinated me.

I blushed at the thought of Grandfather thinking I might become a pirate.

Taking a brief breather to quickly relight his pipe that had gone out through neglect due to his obsession with the story, he blew a few big puffs of smoke and pressed on.

"Not a part of this story, tell you that some other time."

He always answered my questions, often later, and never forgot, except when he figured the answer was too complicated or taboo, then he'd just ignore me.

"Now by this time, Captain Richard had three large fishing schooners of his own operating on the Grand Banks. But he had a sentimental attachment to *The Lucky Shamrock*, took the crew in, and nursed them back to health. Being a wrecked ship adrift on the high seas, by marine law, he was within his right to claim the prize without compensation, but he was fair. He bought the schooner, however for a pittance, repaired it, making it the biggest, at fifty tons, and safest ship in his fleet. In honor of Captain O'Riley, he took over the captain's job, hired all his surviving crew, and she became the pride of the budding Buckle empire.

"By the spring of 1775, three of his eldest sons were already skippering the other three ships. Fish was plentiful, and life was good. During that summer, he was making two bumper trips in *The Lucky Shamrock*, and right beside him were his three young daughters and two wives, who were just as capable, and sometimes more, than the men. His second youngest son was first mate, and his oldest wife was an excellent cook. They worked like clockwork together, one big happy family piling up the riches. Richard was now famous enough to be the subject of both scandalous gossip and envious praise from the Carbonear and St. John's upper-crust society."

Just then, I saw a large single tear ooze from Grandfather's eye, roll down his cheek, and splatter on the floor. I sensed the next step was going to be tragic instead of my fairy-tale ending. He appeared to be summoning the courage to verbalize a disaster. He held his pipe, which had gone out again, in his extended hand without shaking, as if pointing to an invisible person in the room. He was never afraid to cry and had often told me "crying cleanses the soul of your mistakes."

Without blinking or changing his tone of voice, he took a few deep sighs and continued unrelentingly.

"His youngest son, Arnold, from his youngest wife—not really wives, he didn't marry any of them—was not a fisherman but a bookworm like his mother, Sarah. She had sheltered him from hard work because of bouts of coughing caused by asthma, thinking it was TB. Instead, he studied law at the college in St. John's. He always remained behind and helped his mother look after the books and manage the onshore servants. His son was the real brains of the operation, each year identifying shortcomings and suggesting improvements, all based on his skill with numbers. Richard worshiped him, probably because he was schooled, something he missed, but was cautious not to show any affection to anyone except his three wives. It is rumored he treated them like goddesses, could do anything they want with his money, and he would flatten anyone who looked at them the wrong way."

Grandfather relit his pipe and abruptly changed his demeanor, speaking angrily.

"Son, greed only begets more greed. Power and money corrupts. Richard didn't have to take his four ships down to the western banks for a third load that year. His ego took over, he now had illusions of grandeur, a Buckle empire. To somehow compensate for his impoverished youth. A legacy to hand down to his children. Insanity! For a man who had weathered life's sorrows, he'd forgotten pretty bloody fast.

"Tempting fate, on August 13, 1774, *The Lucky Shamrock* led the three other fishing schooners through the narrows of St. John's harbor together, under strict orders to stay within sight of each other, day or night, for safety. Richard's creed had always been 'The family that works together, plays together, prospers together. You are your family's keeper.' He was paranoid about losing any member of his family, he still carried mental scars from years of being alone. He knew losing four ships was unlikely. Besides, there were always numerous other ships fishing the same ground to offer help, including two British navy frigates guarding the fishermen from Yankee raiders.

"On board that ship, my boy, was every member of his family except Sarah and Arnold. He had even suggested they come too, boasting in twenty-two years he never lost a schooner or even a sailor, that both God and the devil were scared of him. His two wives always stayed with him in his cabin, even though other members of his crew didn't like females aboard. 'Bad omens,' they would mumble but too scared to tell him to his face. They believed St. Elmo's fire had hit the main mast twice in the past as a warning for him to mend his sinful ways. Richard was beginning to lose his respect for nature, he was now playing God."

Grandfather became more and more mellow, and once again, his eyes filled with tears. I realized this was not going to be a happy ending for him; my relative, Captain Buckle, and his family were about to become bloodthirsty pirates, robbing other fishing boats to quickly build their empire. I was surprised to see Grandfather go to the mantle and fetch Grandmother's weathered old Bible and place it on his lap, as if to fend off evil spirits. He, like Captain Buckle, was no saint; he also cursed at the drop of a hat.

"With a British frigate within sight guarding the fleet, Richard concentrated on fishing. By pushing himself and his men to the limit, like blacks, by September 7, all four ships were laded to the waterline, every seam filled to the cracks with salted cod. Another bumper crop. Ready to head home. He would now not only be the pride of Carbonear and St. John's but with the British navy viewing his exploits and keeping tally of his harvest and reporting the top performers to the English press, of Dublin and London as well.

"Then in the early morning as he squared his sails, as if by magic, the wind disappeared, and a terrible calm settled over the waters of the Grand Banks. The fog mysteriously lifted, and the sun shone bright. All day, the calm lingered. That night, the moon and stars shone bright and reflected in the water like a mirror. Then it became unusually warm. Balmy weather the likes of which nobody had ever heard of on the ocean there before. All day, the eighth, it lasted, not a draft. Hot as hell, and not a whisper of wind.

"The sailors were nervous, but Richard, taking advantage of the calm, had the sailors from his other three ships use their dories and tow their ships to *The Lucky Shamrock,* where he had them tied together. He then marshaled all the sailors aboard his ship and told them of their reward, a 10 percent increase in their share of the catch for their loyalty and performance. For his family, he promised to take them all to Bermuda in Christmas for a month in *The Lucky Shamrock* to reveal his grandiose plans for their twenty-room mansion there, a headquarters for his new operation, and to view a new fishing schooner being delivered there from Gloucester, a gigantic 120-ton clipper. He planned on cashing in on the lucrative illegal trade in alcohol and tea to the new American colonies in the fishing off-season. All the Buckles were jubilant, they were now in the big league, behind Richard all the way. Richard, right there and then, had his wives and crew organize a grand soiree to celebrate their good fortune on the Grand Banks where they made it."

Grandmother entered and brought Grandfather a strong a cup of tea, which he sipped black. She knew tea calmed him when he became emotional. As he refilled his pipe and relit it, she left and returned with a large glass of hot, freshly scalded cow's milk and a batch of homemade molasses buns.

I was now disappointed. I wanted my ancestors to be fearless marauding scalawags ravaging the Spanish main, but instead, it appeared I was the descendant of some sissy royalty in the Caribbean.

"But that morning, twelve hours earlier, home in Carbonear," Grandfather suddenly recommenced softly, more relaxed and backtracking, "things were different. A disaster was in full progress. During the night, the tide had risen thirty feet above the high-water mark and was flooding all their fishing stages and grub stores. Their wharf was under ten feet of water, it was surrounding their home and just fifty feet from their front door. Thankfully, the house was situated on a high knoll. Most of their purchased winter provisions had been destroyed. The two root cellars had been flooded too, destroying all the vegetables just harvested and stored for the winter. Their low-lying pasture behind them was now a pond with several of their sheep, cows, and goats floating in it.

"Though Arnold and his mother were at first shocked, as if God was flooding the earth again, they were a tough breed. Without a word, with their servants, they organized a major rescue operation to salvage the remaining provisions and animals and boat them across the pond to higher ground. They feared a nor'easter was brewin'. All day, they toiled in the hot sun like pack animals, stopping only to pray for their relatives on the Grand Banks.

"Back on the Grand Banks, the soiree was in full swing. Jugs of moonshine and bottles of Jamaican rum were being merrily passed around. Sailors were singing and dancing arm in arm to reels blaring out from a fiddle, backed up by accordions, mouth organs, and spoons. It was a heavenly panoramic sight too. Torches burning on all the ships lit up the ocean like a Christmas tree. A full moon and a sky full of stars reflected like jewels on a queen's crown in the calm water. Laughter, music, and song intermingled, echoing for miles across the still ocean, attracting dories from other ships, including the British navy frigate. Everybody in bare buff, as warm as in the tropics, hot as hell. The mouthwatering smell of padarah, cod tongues, fish britches frying and an oversized boiling pot of salt beef and cabbage all filled the air for miles. A feast fit for a king."

I could see Grandfather was becoming troubled again as his eyes began to water. I knew him so well, I could guess the outcome before he told it from agony etched in the lines of his eighty-year-old face, and it made me sad too.

"But, my son, it was not to be. They say from the northeast there was a clap of thunder that nearly scared the pants off everyone, even though now, by midnight, they were all drunk, thinking it was a Yankee raider firing on them. Approaching from above was a huge black cloud like a dense fog bank with forked lightning flashing continuously like the fires of hell. Within minutes, a vicious wind squall hit, as biting as the cold Labrador Current in January. The soiree disintegrated into chaos, every sailor scrambled at breakneck speed to untie their dories from *The Lucky Shamrock* and get back to their ships. Rain became torrential, and a dense, icy fog shrouded the ocean like a blanket of death. Instantly, every ship was alone on the ocean, unable to see ten fathoms. Richard, fearing a bloody nor'easter, squared his sails and headed home, blowing his foghorn for his sons to follow.

"Then a strange thing happened. Stumped all the captains. The squall dissipated as quickly as it appeared, but the air was still as frigid as the Arctic. The moon and stars reappeared. It became flat calm again. And within half an hour, the warm weather had returned. Good thing too, for dozens of sailors and fishermen had gotten stranded on the open ocean in their dories without warm clothes, unable to find their ships."

Grandfather seemed relieved and called for Grandmother to bring me more food. Why? That was a surprise, for he had always reprimanded me for eating between meals. But I was now too engrossed in the story, telling him I wasn't hungry, urging him to continue; my imagination was now working overtime. I wanted to hear my happy ending in which we were bloodthirsty marauding pirates, the scourge of the Caribbean, notorious buccaneers feared in all the world's oceans.

"Frightened sober by the ghastly squall and their narrow escape, everyone turned in to sleep and prepare for tomorrow's breeze, which they knew wasn't far off. Within an hour, everyone was sleeping soundly, serenaded by the long, gentle swell, which was gradually increasing, and the effects of the alcohol, dreaming of being home with their families for the rest of the winter."

Grandfather made a deep sigh, put his pipe down, and became more somber and melancholic than I envisaged a tough sane man should be. He spoke to me directly, a stern warning to be heeded earnestly.

"What happened next, my son, was a lesson in humility. Not to tempt Mother Nature, you'll lose. In this world, you're just a spit in the bucket. Richard was about to learn how fast fate can change one's life in the twinkling of an eye, that money and fame is fleeting.

"The hurricane hit without warning like the hammer of Thor. Wind never heard of on the banks. Over two hundred miles an hour, some said later, and more. Fog and mist, thick as pea soup. Rain poured from the heavens in buckets. Dories on the water went airborne. The ship's rigging ripped to shreds. In a few hours, every ship on the Grand Banks and western banks had floundered. Some say over two hundred. And the British navy frigates didn't escape the devil's fury either. Every sailor and fisherman died to the last man, most still in their bunks, not knowing what happened and without even a prayer. Ships became kindling, floating debris, driftwood. It littered the beaches, along with decaying bodies, for months afterward. Thousands of hardworking innocent people wiped off the face of the earth, in one sweep of God's terrible wrath."

Thousands? I was startled, left breathless at my sudden change of fortunes. Tears streamed down my face. All my imaginary, tough, seafaring pirates were dead without a fighting chance. I wondered where I came from.

"And that's only half of it. The hurricane slammed into the land with the same ferocity. Everything within a hundred yards of the beach was obliterated. Not only fishing wharves and moored skiffs, but homes, churches, everything blown to smithereens. Half the vegetables still in the ground. Animals and people died together. The fury of the Lord was awesome. Flung like matchsticks hundreds of feet up the cliffs. Don't tempt the Lord thy God, my son."

Grandfather's vivid description of God terrified me. Grandmother always told me he was a loving God who forgave my mistakes.

Hundreds of feet?

Our house was basically on the beach, and I had seen plenty of nor'easters and knew how vicious they could be.

"The calm was the eye of the hurricane, some said, but I know—"

"What happened to our ancestors Sarah and Arnold?" I interjected, disappointed, not wanting to hear any more destruction, already traumatized by an oversupply of mayhem and death. "We came from a weak, sick person?"

Grandfather, recognizing my shock and dismay, answered more kindly, patting me on the head.

"No, my boy. Arnold wasn't weak. He didn't have asthma either. This damn 'baccy," he said, showing me his smoking pipe. "Soon as he stopped the bloody habit, his affliction disappeared. And most of the smoke came from his relatives when he was a kid." Grandfather became authoritative again and lectured me. "Don't smoke this garbage, my son, will kill you."

I thought that amusing since he smoked like a tilt, was in his eighties, and still going strong. It cheered me up a bit.

"With the frigid Newfoundland winter approaching and no food, shelter, chances of survival for Sarah and Arnold was bleak. With Richard's money and friends, they made it to St. John's that winter, and next spring to England, Arnold attended Oxford there and got a law degree. He then moved back to St. John's and started his practice helping the poor fishermen fight against the oppressive fish merchants. He married a preacher's daughter and had four sons. His mother lived with him to a ripe old age, never married, but she lived a long and prosperous life. Mostly because of Arnold's success."

"Our name is Bessey," I challenged him. "Why not Buckle? We were Normans."

Grandfather grinned and patted me on the head joyfully. He seldom smiled. "That's another story. Tell you later. I didn't say he had no youngsters by other women. He was his father's son, you know."

I was still unhappy with my history. I was the offspring of some sissy lawyer's daughter. Grandfather, reading my displeasure, went on, somewhat disappointed himself.

"In England, Arnold researched his family tree. Seems we're no more than bloody seafaring Vikings who settled temporarily in Normandy."

I smiled. Now we were getting somewhere. I was the descendant of a bloodthirsty Viking raider! I was happy. My dream had come true.

I was a pirate after all.

Some twenty years ago, researching my family line, I was astounded to learn that my grandfather's so-called fairy tale was actually true, although Richard Buckle was not the correct name, and vividly recalled him telling me this tragic story of that very Newfoundland Hurricane. However, it is a sad legacy that such a hurricane that had cost 4,200 lives is lost in the annals of Newfoundland's history.

I also realized my grandfather must have been a direct descendant of Richard Buckle. My grandfather was big, blond, blue-eyed, aggressive, and rumored to be a notorious womanizer.

I am now proud to be his offspring—a pirate.

Chronicle 2

Angels of Death

Religion, the world's most arrogant form of ignorance,
is the bane of society.

This dramatization of the Spanish flu in Labrador is dedicated to Martha Joshua of Uivak, who, as a seven-year-old Inuit, survived the nightmarish ordeal of being alone for five weeks in -30°C weather, living only on hard bread and snow, as every member of her family lay dead around her, being savagely eaten by hungry sled dogs that sometimes attacked her.

God's emissaries of the Moravian Church came to Labrador in the 1760s and established a mission at Makkovik to "civilize the indigenous heathens" of the coast—first reported as exceptionally friendly by Basque fishermen—who noted these "wild savages" who had no written language and who had not yet discovered the wheel, had an innate curiosity for foreign innovations, and showed undue respect for those who knew how to implement these new methods, making conditions ripe for an influx of Europe's overzealous religious soul savers to embark on *missions* to enlighten them of the ways of the white man's loving and merciful God. And, naturally, missionaries were sponsored by business ventures. Thus began the forced evangelization of the Inuit, and the decline of an ancient people and its culture.

First, the age-old Inuit practice of equality for men and women living communally in extended family units or bands, intermarrying and sharing the chores and caring for each other was considered unhealthy and immoral by Christians, and they were urged—more correctly, coerced—into giving up their nomadic lifestyle and to settle down in single-family housing units in organized communities, near Moravian churches, of course, for better control and surveillance. A proven divide-and-conquer mentality, there simply being too much strength in communal living.

Second, the eating of raw meats was frowned upon and considered savage; thus, the passive Inuit gave up their healthy traditional diets and, as directed, ate the salty, canned, sugary processed foods, conveniently supplied for them from the church trading posts in exchange for furs and fish.

Supplied with white man's firearms, thus began the mass slaughter of the several coastal species of animals for the clothing and hats of the Europe's elite. And those unable to pay their bills were indentured as servants and sometimes shipped overseas to be exhibited in zoos and freak shows; such was the case of the devout Christian family of Abraham Ulrikab, who, in Europe without their traditional family support, died of abuse, despair, or diseases within a year. Their transgression was a £15 debt at the Moravian trading post.

The consequences were immediate. Robbed of their traditional source of food and clothing, they starved, froze to death, or died of despair. The *cultured* food in conjunction with a sedentary lifestyle brought diabetes, high blood pressure, and heart disease; and close association with God's missionaries brought whooping cough, measles, tuberculosis, scarlet fever, polio, smallpox, and every known form of silent, invisible killer of the civilized world. And of course, alcohol—the blood of Jesus—first introduced by the priests in communion, and syphilis, probably introduced by the same priests to the obedient youth just after communion, who were culturally indoctrinated into respecting their elders.

The Moravians, with their main priority—business—taken care of, could now move on to God and spirituality. The Inuit was required to give up their earthly heathen gods with their dark-age belief that everything on earth had a spirit and demanded respect, the idea that no person could own land, and that one should take only as much from nature as needed for survival. Veneration of Sedna, their sea goddess, who lived beneath the waters and who provided most of their marine animals, their main source of food, was openly ridiculed, an effective tactic of control in the religious world for humbling those dissidents who could not read or write. It became sacrilege just to mention the names of any Inuit gods or goddesses, whom their ancestors had worshiped for some ten thousand years. Schools were compulsory, and all children had to attend to be "civilized" and learn proper English etiquette. As a result, children were separated from their families for some ten months a year and subjected to severe discipline, a trait foreign to free-spirited nomads. Even their language was considered offensive; speaking Inuktitut was forbidden in public. To add insult to injury, the very name of their race was being deleted; they were now Eskimos. Communities now had English names. Children were forced to take Christian names. It was ethnic cleansing systematically carried out in the name of God.

Awed by with the white man's superior knowledge and power and brutally subjected to their strict legal codes, the Inuit were soon made to feel like an inferior race. Those who objected became criminals in their own land with penalties enforced by foreigners with superior weapons. In return, they were guaranteed that the Christian God, who lived invisibly up in the heavens, would love and care for them if they converted and followed. And follow they did, like lambs to the slaughter.

Literally!

And God mercilessly collected his harvest by the thousands, young and old alike, victims of the Inuit's loving and forgiving nature. Of the estimated six thousand Inuit roaming the coast when the Moravians arrived, without immunity, 70 percent of the population had been eradicated by 1918. And of the remaining 1,800 souls, 30 percent would die of the Spanish flu in just two months in the fall of 1918.

In 1918, Newfoundland, though being an independent country since 1855, still imported most of its provisions from mother England but, with fish as its main commodity, traded mostly with the eastern Boston *S*tates, where the misnamed Spanish flu is believed to have originated. And all trade went through the influential Newfoundland fish merchants in the capital, St. Johns.

St. John's was also the chief port of entry for soldiers returning from the war in Europe, where on October 30, 1918, a ship arrived with an insidious Halloween treat, a cargo of death disguised as mild cases of flu in just three infected soldiers. Within two weeks, the city had a full-blown epidemic on its hands, Spanish flu. Schools, churches, theaters, and other public places were closed, and all afflicted homes were quarantined. With hospitals overflowing, vacant buildings were converted into makeshift clinics, and with all the professional doctors and nurses overseas repairing the mangled bodies of the trench soldiers protecting Europe's feuding royalty, medics and untrained personnel were left to attend to the sick. Medicine was in short supply or nonexistent. Once contacted, mortality rate was high, nearly 1 percent.

In spite of the pandemic being well-known and monitored by the Newfoundland government, who had mandatory restrictions in place across the island, the wealthy fish merchants controlled the shipping, and there being few roads, the distribution of all goods to even the tiniest outport on the island or in Labrador was by coastal ships, and merchants could not allow death to get in the way of profit. In fact, government policy was dictated by the rich fish merchants. Workers had no rights, and even activists like Croaker were constrained by the business elite.

Terrianiak Agluka, known by all as Terri, was a traditional Inuit from Uivaq, Labrador, and one of the first indigenous people to engage in business as lackeys for the white man, acting on their behalf as traders in furs and fish for manufactured goods. Money was discouraged, strictly barter. Money would bring independence and give influence to the ignorant masses.

On October 20, Terri boarded the SS *Sagona,* one of the winter provisioning ships out of St. John's from Okak to Hebron, to do his monthly enumeration on pelts and fish and, it being the last excursion of the year before winter freeze up, to spend a week of socializing with his extended family. His business dealings, combined with his easy, outgoing personality, led him to associate with nearly every family in each of the communities on the coast, as well as the all the captains and officers of the supply ships.

On Terri's trip north, he met Ingmar Hanson, his Swedish friend and counterpart, just back from Europe, who was expediently employed by the Moravian brotherhood. Sweden, being a neutral country in the war, permitted him to travel unobstructed across borders and to act as a broker for the wholesaling of Inuit animal pelts to the largest multinational furriers of Europe. With the war raging and winters frigid, warm clothes were in high demand. Plus, furs were in vogue; the slogan of the day was "think mink" but aptly applied to all furs.

Their frequent meetings, typically held each month on board ship, where they invariably shared a double first-class berth, usual deteriorated into a drunken soiree; both were borderline alcoholics. Their commotion often attracted others eager to share in their free drinks, which typically were bottles of Jamaican rum freely passed around until empty, and anyone considered a *real man* drank straight from the bottle.

Their party lasted for several days as the SS *Sagona* crawled its way up the Labrador coast, stopping at every port to unload its cargo and take on furs. And in each hamlet, Terri and Ingmar went ashore to offer drinks to their customers in appreciation.

On the day before the SS *Sagona* reached Hebron, Ingmar became ill. This, for some unknown reason, caused the captain to become extremely agitated and deeply troubled, ordering anyone with even a mild flu to be quarantined in the wretched quarters of third class, including Ingmar, a rich, influential person. This irritated Terri since the captain, though normally an amiable fellow, was also a very heavy drinker. And more, the captain, Terri's longtime friend, severely reprimanded him for his excessive drinking and supplying alcohol to others. But most puzzling and troubling was the captain's accusation that he was endangering people's lives. He was baffled—he, a man who would never hurt a fly. He could not remotely fathom how his friend could be so secretive about a simple cold.

Arriving at Hebron, Terri felt abnormally tired with a touch of chill. He visited the local clinic and was fortunate enough to encounter Dr. Grenfell, who was in town making his final fall rounds on the coast and who was due to leave the following day. The doctor assured Terri that he had only a common cold caused by being overworked and prescribed rest, to refrain from alcohol, and to go to church.

Terri was not a subscriber to the white man's religion, quite the opposite. He practiced the traditional Inuit culture, worshiped Sedna, ate raw meat and fish when alone, and wore warm homemade fur clothing. But unable to complete his business due to Ingmar's illness and thankful that he was in good health, plus it being Sunday, he took the good doctor's advice and went to the church service to greet the congregation and possibly conjure up more business.

While socializing with his extended family in Hebron, the captain of the SS *Sagona* relayed Terri an urgent messenger that his friend Ingmar was fatally ill, unlikely to survive, and that he must avoid contact with people at all cost. Stunned by the sudden turn of events and disappointed in the captain's mysterious directive, on October 27, he took the last ship of the year, the SS *Harmony,* back to Okak. While on board, out of protocol as a trader, he met with the crew and the ship's passengers but did no partying, consumed no alcohol, ate only his traditional foods, and otherwise stayed alone in his berth practicing his tribal remedies for colds, a steeped juniper berry juice potion and lots of Labrador tea. He was distressed and confused about his friend Ingmar. He noticed nobody on the SS *Harmony* had the flu except him.

By the time he arrived back at Okak on November 4, he was back to normal. There was no flu in Okak, so he figured it was just seasonal cold, not worthy of mention, and stayed with friends there for a few days before returning home to Uivaq.

Terri's association with the missionaries had made him affluent enough to have white contractors build him build a large house complete with all the modern amenities of life. He was the envy of his neighbors, with whom he shared some of his good fortune. He was content with his lot in life, but most of all, like most Inuit, he was a fun-loving family man who was extremely proud of his three sons and two daughters, who were studying at the missionary boarding school up in Natuk. They were smart and doing him proud learning to read and write. His little schooling had worked well for him, and he could imagine them assuming control of his lucrative business when old enough. But he was distressed at their loss of native culture and paid a local elder to indoctrinate them, much to the dismay of the Moravians, but they were reluctant to expel their best paying students.

Terri prized his ancestral ways; he loved the outdoors, and after a summer of mostly processed foods and three more days of much the same at home from his converted wife and with his stash of smoke-dried fish having been depleted, it was more than he could tolerate. The next day, with three friends, they set out with their sleds and teams of huskies to gather their winter supply of caribou, which, like seal, was Terri's favorite food when eaten raw. The caribou proved elusive, and his two friends returned home after a week, both feeling sick; but he persevered and finally located the animals.

A week later, as he happily pulled up his home with his sled laden with two dressed frozen caribou, he was puzzled no crowds came running to congratulate him. Finding nobody inside, he checked few neighbors' homes with the same result. Being caribou season, he guessed the tiny hamlet's eighteen people were all away in hunting camps. He stayed the night, stored his caribou, and next day headed for his wife's sister's house in Okak, where she often stayed to avoid being alone. However, with her being a devout Christian, in this instance, it was more likely she went there to celebrate Christmas, a practice he despised. He respected her faith, but having to journey such a long distance in winter weather to collect her made him very upset.

Arriving at Okak, he was confronted with a horrific sight, a scene straight out of the white man's hell. More than a two hundred bodies littered the snowy ground around the houses, as if tossed outside like garbage. Some frozen into the ice, some mostly covered in snow, others partly eaten by roaming dogs, all with white, glassy faces staring into space. The place was a deserted wasteland. And not a living soul in sight! It looked as if the angels of death had smote the Inuit heathens as he often heard the Moravian preacher thunder from the white man's Bible. He had an eerie feeling of impending doom.

Terri went from house to house, but nobody would permit him to enter. Finally, he met Tulugaq, the community retarded woman, who explained that nearly everyone had died of a disease called the Spanish flu, and the authorities blamed him for spreading it. He just stood flabbergasted, shocked speechless, staring blankly at her. But crazy Tulugaq went on mercilessly, saying the ground was too hard to bury them, and even so, there was nobody left to do the work, all the men were dead, that Uviak wasn't deserted, their dead spirits were still there, and there was nobody left alive in Sillutalik either. As she droned on endlessly, Terri was alone with his thoughts. He recalled his friend, Ingmar, who had just returned from Europe. He wondered if he were in Spain and contracted the flu there. He now figured the captain blamed him too. Was he really the carrier? Did he actually kill all these people? It was all too ghastly to comprehend. He was frozen in time.

Tulugaq's next statement jolted Terri back to reality and stunned him even more with the revelation that his wife and his wife's sister's family were all dead too, as was all his children in Hebron. He felt numb. Unable to process the truth, he finally found his tongue and assailed Tulugaq, accused her of being a lying retard. It wasn't possible, he rationalized; he had been away for only two weeks. But the stark reality was displayed all around him. The final blow came when she told him she didn't get sick because the Moravian preacher ordered people to stay away from her because she was possessed by the devil.

Terri was a tough man and no stranger to disaster, but for the next hour, he sat in a snowbank, slowly drank a bottle of rum, and cried, reliving his past with his family and pondering his future without them, as Tulugaq talked incessantly about death, serializing the number of deaths from each community. Finally accepting his fate, he stoically set about the task of burying the dead. In the next two weeks, with the help of Tulugaq who convinced other women to help, they piled firewood, poured gas on it, and made a massive bonfire to thaw the frozen ground beneath. By January 7, 1919, a large pit had been hacked out, thirty-two feet long and eight feet deep, and 204 of Okak's residents were buried together in one mass grave, side by side, stacked like firewood. And just as Tulugaq had said, every man in the community was dead.

To prevent the flu from spreading, the remaining fifty-nine female survivors burned all the houses and everything within them, sparing only the clothes on their back, which they fumigated with smoke from burning birch bark, and then, with only a week's supply of smoked caribou in their backpacks, young and old alike, all headed out into the vicious -30°C weather, trekking hundreds of miles to Hebron, Natuk, and Hopedale.

Terri reluctantly headed back home alone to his beautiful empty home in Uivaq, pondering why he was spared. Arriving in early morning, he noticed dozens of dogs fighting over food in front of the Joshua household, which he soon discovered to be a child's body.

He dispersed the dogs with his whip and entered. Inside he found seven-year-old Martha Joshua, alive and well, in a house without heat, water, or food, and dressed warmly in her sealskin clothes, eating hard bread and snow. It had been five weeks since she had last seen a person alive. She was the only person alive in the community.

Two months later, the government of Newfoundland in St. John's, now satisfied the epidemic had now played itself out, requisitioned the Moravian missionary headquarters in Nain for a body count. The wireless reply read:

> Per your request. Inventory of dead: Spanish flu: Nain; Labrador
> White Christians: 9 dead from all areas.
> Eskimos: Hebron: 86 of 100 dead.
> Hebron area: 150 of 220 dead.
> Otlik: 13 of 18 dead.
> Sillutalik: 40 of 45 dead.
> Okak: 204 out of 263 dead; burnt town; all left.
> Will relay count for other areas as reported in.

Okak, before the pandemic, was the largest and most prosperous Inuit settlement on the Labrador coast. In just two months, it ceased to exist. Less than 1 percent of the white people in Labrador died compared to a full 35 percent the coastal Inuit population, and of those who survived, most suffered the rest of their lives from respiratory diseases or heart problems.

Yet in of spite of the horrendous death toll, a mission preacher in his first sermon after the pandemic made this statement in front of just twenty destitute remaining Inuit: "This should be a lesson to all Eskimos. The flu was but an example God's wrath on your people because of your lascivious, sinful ways."

Many humanitarian organizations after 1918, including the famous International Grenfell Association headquartered at St. Anthony, tried unsuccessfully to shut down the powerful Moravian missions, advocating the Inuit could best run their own affairs, but the power of religion was stronger.

The impact of the Spanish flu and the cost of paying for mother England's war would force Newfoundland into bankruptcy, in which it would never recover, and lead back to commission government. And after another of Europe's wars, in which England again milked its colonies of its money, resources, and people, England made a secret deal with Canada to accept Newfoundland as its tenth province, an insidious political maneuver to avoid having to repay its war reparation bills, as Canada had already forgiven England's war debt.

After confederation with Canada and the advent of mass media, the Grenfell Association changed tactics and lobbied the federal government with the frequent airing of dramatic radio stories and television pictures of inhuman Inuit living conditions. Under siege, finally, on Easter Monday 1959, Rev. Siegfried Hettasch conceded defeat with the following infamous statement: "I see *no other way* than to suggest the mission withdraw from Hebron this summer."

He failed to mention that the Moravian Mission's decision was the result of exhaustive consultation with the federal government in which they received a lucrative settlement for their cooperation and for the purchase of all their assets above market value.

Then the Canadian government, like the Moravians and the Newfoundland government earlier, missed the point again. The Inuit nomadic lifestyle was forgotten, and once more, they were herded together and resettled into ever larger communities, forcing dependency on social welfare programs, resulting into further loss of dignity, stigma, and alienation; and with most of the population being young and restless, they turned to drugs.

It wasn't until 2005 that the Newfoundland government under Premier Danny Williams made a formal apology to the Inuit and the Innu for their gross mistreatment and, in conjunction with the government of Canada, afforded them autonomy over half of Labrador, their own land named Nunatsiavut, *our beautiful homeland* in Inuktitut. The government of Nunatsiavut is now responsible for health, education, and cultural affairs to preserve the Inuit culture and language, as well as the caretaker of their environment. They were also afforded a stake in their land's mineral resources.

But even then, there was an ulterior motive. Lessons learned from Voisey's Bay mining projects, having been stalled for years by aboriginal land claims, led the government to admit defeat and join forces with the Inuit in order to get approval for the development of the lower Churchill power project, which is also native land.

Step-by-step, the indigenous people clawed back their own land but at a horrendous cost. At least now, though, with mass media, it is in the open without the facade of being carried out in the name of God.

Some 250 years after the first subjugation by the Moravians, the Inuit finally had a home again.

Much positive has been written by missionaries about their noble Christian deeds in bringing justice and truth to the Inuit of Labrador. Most explorers proclaim their piety, using misleading words like *discovery* and *humanitarian* when justifying their work in America for the glory of God, but the stark truth speaks for itself; it was for gold and land. The Inuit were not lost; they were a resourceful, independent people who survived the unforgiving Arctic for six thousand years, and their gods were just as definable as the white man's. History is what the winners write; the past is what happened and is usually written by the critics or interred with the bones of the victims. Never confuse justice with truth.

Religion, the world's most arrogant form of ignorance, is the bane of society.

Chronicle 3

The Saga of the Ribbed Ghost Ship

"Don't mock wat yuh don't understand. Not everyt'ing is learned from books."

"B'yes, if youse goin' bakeapplein' down L'Anse aux Meadows, leave before duckish, you know der's a spirit ship der in Black Duck Brook," Walter Taylor warned the berry-picking party as they prepared their utensils. He tapped the tobacco ashes from his pipe on the stove fender and added pensively, "Seen it wit' me own two eyes, many times."

Everyone willingly nodded their agreement.

Walter Taylor was well up in his eighties and a well-respected member of Ha Ha Bay. Had led his family successfully through many trials and tribulations, had many misfortunes in his time, and few questioned his hard-earned credentials.

Ready to return to college after a hectic summer and needing a reprieve from the drudgery of fishing, I quickly decided to tag along with the group to pick bakeapples; it would supplement my meager education fund. I didn't believe in spirits, but I was born with an inquisitive nature and overactive mind. Being near the top in the college debating club, the idea of a spine-tingling ghost yarn from local folklore intrigued me and would provide some much needed data for a unique essay. Knowing my mentality, the group was leery of the idea of my tagging along, figuring a rogue member would be counterproductive.

I decided to explore further.

"Is this ghost a Dorset Eskimo or a Beothuk?" I asked seriously, trying not to sound facetious.

All stopped and stared piercingly at me. I had confirmed their fears; I would indeed be a troublemaker. Walter stopped de-ashing his pipe, stood up, faced me, slowly refilled his pipe, relit it, then spoke with a reverence that startled me. "I know youse smart, but don't t'ink you knows every'ting. Me dear fadder—God bless 'is soul—and 'is fadder 'fore 'im, and 'is fadder 'fore dat, seen dat ship dere in Black Duck Brook. I dare yuh to wait 'lone 'round duckish wen da strange mist rises o'er the marshes. 'Twill prove if youse da man yuh t'ink youse is. Youse fadder done it. Nothin' scared 'im. Seen it too. Da proof of da bangbelly is in da eatin'."

I was taken aback and left speechless at the subtle reprimand but, more so, puzzled at his unorthodox and somber challenge. Before I could accept his dare, the other members of the party had already decided that I had been deleted. No need to intimidate the ghost.

"The brook is too shallow for a ship," I informed him as courteously as possible, trying delicately to influence the group. "Must be a small dory?"

He shook the stem of his pipe at me and, in the same solemn, determined mood, responded, "Don't mock wat yuh don't understand, me son. Not everyt'ing is learned from books. 'Tis not flat bottomed. 'Tis a long narrow ribbed ship. Sixty foot I'd say. Nuttin' like our dories. Strange kind. High stem and stern. Garge Decker says one sail in da center. Didn't see dat dough. Goes up da brook like a 'aze, a dank, dark fog. Sea-fearin' creatures wit 'ard-lookin' faces in it. Like in da Good Book. The devil's raven always flies 'long wit' it."

For a sensible, tough, weather-beaten fisherman, he spoke with a strange, unnerving convection. His meticulous detailing of such a bizarre, homespun fireplace fable impressed me. I stared at him blankly with a surprised, puzzled expression on my face.

"Forget bakeapplein'. Youse smart, you kin write 'bout it," he went on. Then turning and staring directly at the others, leaving no doubt he wanted them to permit me go along, he noted, "Can't read 'n write, yuh know. Only knows w'at I 'ears an' sees. Needs proof."

Disappointed faces showed the others silently disagreed, but no one objected to his inference. Most likely because it was his boat they were using.

"It's late summer. Likely an optical illusion, a mirage caused by a weather inversion," I suggested cautiously, grateful for his approval.

"Don't 'ave yuh brains, me son," he responded in the same grave tone, "but at my age, yuh knows a weat'er fairy from a ghost ship."

I decided to back off, not wanting to offend him.

The others, now verbally agitated at my *ignorance* for questioning such a long-standing locally accepted phenomenon, urged Uncle Walt to reconsider. I could sense that they were nervous of my stalking a ghost. I also had a strange feeling that Walter's concern was genuine; a desire for me to go was not to teach me some lesson or out of revenge for a few brownie points but to make me appreciate that education was not wisdom, that not all learning came from books, that folklore had its merits, that there was indeed an anomaly there and my brains could solve it. I was grateful for his persistence.

"Has anyone else seen this apparition?" I asked as the berry pickers began to file out the door with their buckets and nunny bags, complaining I was a smart-arse, a bloody nuisance, and should instead be sent packing back to college where I belonged.

Walter's unusual eagerness to talk candidly about spirits, plus his insistence for me to investigate, fascinated me even more.

"Yaaaaas, me son," he responded enthusiastically, stretching out the word. "Garge Decker lives down dere. As' 'im. Seen it 'undreds a times. Showed it to me. Always jist 'fore dark. Comes queerlike. Rises from nowhere. Sometimes 'ears screeches. Women. Youngsters too."

"Where does it go?" I queried hurriedly, anxious to run along and catch the others who were trying to lose me.

"Always da same spot. Stops right 'bove dem t'ree or four 'ummocks on the ground." He paused and handed me a pair of binoculars. "Sush along now. 'Tis a warm ca'm day. 'Twill get foggy later. Should see it dis evenin'. Tell dem ta get back 'ere 'fore midnight."

"Thank you, sir," I offered, rushing out the door without a bucket or a lunch, fearing I had been left behind.

It was a bright sunny as the old six-horsepower Atlantic engine chugged the old thirty-foot cod-fishing boat along over the flat, calm water. Blatantly obvious I was not a welcome member of the party, I sat quietly alone on the cuddy admiring the heavenly reflections mirrored in the flat, calm ocean, the occasional porpoise or whale surfacing, the screeching seagulls overhead, and terns splashing around us.

Shane Dawe came forward and crudely barked me some of his practical wisdom through a bout of smoker's cough, hacking, and spitting into the ocean, "None of your shenanigans, mind you. Stay with the group, away from the brook. And don't go near George Decker's hay shack on the beach there. That's where the ribbed ghost ship comes ashore."

A more daring challenge was hard to imagine. I remained quiet and smiled. It irritated him.

"You'll get left behind," he warned, going back aft. "We'll leave just before dark." Noticing no nunny bag, he added, "You got no food?"

"The ghost will feed me," I joked.

"Bloody smart-arse," he mumbled under his breath.

By 11:00 a.m., the boat was moored in a secluded little cove called Caplin Gulch, and we all hustled together toward the berry patch but pretty soon became dispersed as competition to find the riper, denser patches ensued. After two hours, my tolerance for picking bakeapples—most of which I ate—had been reached. My mind was on the ghost ship, and I began to inch my way toward George Decker's hay shack on Black Duck Brook. At four, a cloud shaded the sun, and with nobody in sight, I headed for the beach among the debris and driftwood for camouflage then made a beeline dash to the shack, which was somewhat concealed behind the lay of the land.

A quick inspection revealed it was a simple but sturdy old wooden building where hay was stored after the fall harvest. There was a little loft, where someone had slept, with a window opening offering an unobstructed view of the brook and the ocean. A dozen or so head of cattle, all with bells, and a small herd of sheep roamed leisurely nearby. The grassy marsh was alive with the chirping of songbirds. I strolled for a hundred yards up the tiny creek, stumbling over slippery rocks, pushing through tall grasses and withies. Nothing unusual. It was a relatively wide, deep ravine with large boulders for the tiny creek that trickled through it. Well sheltered from the ocean by the withies, it trapped the sun's heat.

No tall ships here, I deduced sarcastically, not enough water to quench the grazing animals thirst. I then meandered casually through the tall leathery grasses toward the four hummocks that Walter had urged me to investigate, searching for anything abnormal or paranormal. Nothing. Just irregular glacial deposits overgrown with tall grasses. The phantom ship didn't have far to travel, I pondered mockingly, only a few hundred feet from the beach. Folklore at its best.

After trudging over and closely surveying every inch of the terrain for two hours, my curiosity was quenched. No ghosts or goblins but plenty of red ripe gooseberries on tall bushes. I ate my fill. It was hot and still early. Nothing to do, I succumbed to boredom, went back to the hayloft in the cool, lay down and soon fell asleep.

I awoke at dusk just to see the sun's rays being dispersed through the cracks in the wall. The cowbells had stopped. No lambs were baaing or birds chirping. All was silent. I kneeled up and peered out through the window opening just as the red fireball lowered itself into the placid ocean illuminating a white boat some miles away heading toward Ha Ha Bay.

I jumped up, stunned. My party had actually deserted me as threatened. For a time, I angrily pondered their drastic action, appalled they could have been so cold and callous. Were they vindictive or scared? After a brief bout of frustration, I relaxed and accepted my fate, trapped until morning. *Well, I'll have company, the ghost ship will visit me at least*, I mused sarcastically.

I surveyed my meager survival resources. A half quart of bakeapples, lots of clean drinking water in the creek, and plenty of hay to keep warm, relative to my destitute background, more than adequate. But the thought of walking thirty miles on pebbly beaches tomorrow with low sneakers both depressed and angered me.

I watched the sun dip below the horizon as the land began to cool rapidly. In the next two hours, a gentle, soft sea mist emerged from where the little creek dribbled into the ocean and met the incoming tide. Stealthily, the mist meandered inland up the creek bed. Separate patches of land fog also began to form o'er the heated rocks in the ravine as the warm air met the soft breeze from the sea. The sea mist progressed reluctantly up the creek until it merged fully with the land fog, creating a fresh blanket of clean white haze that hovered above the creek, illuminated by a full moon and a canopy of stars, making it clearly recognizable as typical land fog.

Just off the seashore, another bank of dark, denser ocean fog was forming in patches, creating a kaleidoscope of forms and shapes in various shades of grey in the bright moonlight as air currents moved and skewered it, pushing it onshore. I could feel its chilly sting.

I watched curiously like a starstruck kid trying to identify discernable shapes, specifically ghost ships, in the clouds but to no avail. By eleven o'clock, the dense, dark sea fog had intermingled completely with the inland fog and mist making my childish game academic.

"No ghosts or goblins tonight," I told myself. "Get some sleep, moron, you have a long hike tomorrow on an empty stomach and weak ankles."

I was drifting off to sleep again when a deep voice thundered in the distance, breaking the eerie silence. For a second, I thought my overeating berries was causing me to hallucinate. I listened intently, the sound of my heartbeat increasing in intensity with the voice as it drew progressively closer. I gazed squint-eyed through the little opening into a clear, bright moonlit night and saw a massive figure, a giant, emerging out of the large dark patch of sea fog near where the brook flowed into the ocean. The exact spot where Walter told had me was the source of the ghost. I tried to call back, but the words wouldn't come; I was breathless. My throat was dry. My heart suddenly stopped.

"It's just a night mirage, Ed," I chastised myself with more conviction than I felt, quickly regaining control of my runaway emotions. "The atmospheric conditions are right." Rationally, it was the only possible explanation, an inversion of a person some miles away.

But the ghastly sight continued, slowly floating directly toward the shack, mumbling some undecipherable mantra to itself. It stopped abruptly at the entrance, stood erect, a giant frame filling the doorway, a Herculean statue silhouetted against the full moon with light beams diffusing around its edges.

"Anybody 'ere?" it croaked with a volume that vibrated the wooden building.

When it moved, the bright moonbeams reflected off the wildest, toughest, grainiest, weather-beaten face I could have ever imagined, and I stared down into his squinting eyes.

He rasped again, more civilized this time, "Is yuh Ed?" I still could not find my voice. He tried again. "Did yuh see the ribbed ship?"

"No," I finally answered pensively after a long pause and almost in a whisper.

"Is yuh Ed?" he reiterated.

"Yes," I managed meekly, unsure of what was about to happen next. "And you, sir?"

"Garge Decker me b'ye. 'Ad a good mind to scare yuh. 'Eard yuh wouldn't dat easy to scare, doh, like yuh fadder I s'pose. Knows yuh fadder."

Scared? That was an understatement. Terrified was only mildly accurate. Still trembling like a leaf. But my stubborn ego would not permit me to admit it.

I gave a sigh of relief, felt my pulse return, and scurried down the ladder to greet him.

"Yuh cowardly friends looked fer yuh. Warned me yuh was 'eadstrong. Knows wat dat's like meself. 'Most likely in the shack,' day said, 'lookin' fer spirits.' Told me to collect yuh. Scared buggers. Says yuh 'ad no grub. Come and bunk at our 'ouse da night. Don't fancy yuh walk 'ome, doh."

Nor did I!

As we trekked back to his home, he unhurriedly told me the saga of the ribbed ship with such sincerity and gusto that at times I glanced nervously behind to assure myself that we were not being stalked by the phantom. At his home, a delicious cooked meal was already waiting for me on the table. Seeing my interest in the supernatural, as we ate, he narrated almost nonstop about restless roaming headless spirits, church apparitions complete with graveyards full of walking dead, and mournful sounds from below, strange happenings in the mist on the marshes, unexplainable weather lights lurking beyond the harbor shoals and reefs, washed-up giant krakens and grotesque sea monsters, bloodcurdling screams from the gulches, prophetic dreams of foreboding disasters, ghosts guarding buried pirate treasure stashes hidden around the secluded coves and bays.

His yarns were an endless saga.

Later, as we sat around the crackling woodstove, he smoked his pipe and continued unabated with local shipwrecks, heart-wrenching losses, horrendous tragedies, all fused together and in the same acceptant "that's life, I seen it all, me b'ye" tone of voice. He was a treasure trove of legends. His knowledge was astounding. I enjoyed every second of his company. A more informative, obliging, and kinder man I had never met. His appearance was hardened steel, but his heart was as soft as gold.

Next morning, after a hardy breakfast of fish and brewis, his wife packed a sack of food for my jaunt home as he detailed all the shortcuts and pitfalls to ease my journey. Upon leaving, he encouraged, "Da ribbed ship ain't 'urt nobody. You'll be all right, youse like yuh fadder."

Twelve hours later, I arrived back in Ha Hay Bay on sore feet, sweaty, exhausted, and riled, ready to heap scorn on the cowardly traitors.

Two years later, I boarded the local ferryboat that couriered mail around the coast from St. Anthony to Ha Ha Bay—there being no roads. It was a small decked motorboat owned by my next-door neighbor, Scott Taylor. He was ecstatic. Had a pressing yarn to tell me. Enthusiastically, he urged me below deck to introduce me to his two most famous passengers. A stern-looking, deep-suntanned tall blond man and his wife, equally tanned.

"Ed, you remember the time Shane Dawe stranded you for searching for the ribbed ghost ship?" he related excitedly. "Bakeapple picking down L'Anse aux Meadows, a couple of years ago?"

"How could I forget?" I retorted, "I had to walk thirty miles back home because the stupid moron believed Walt Taylor and George Decker saw a ribbed ghost ship in dry Black Duck Brook."

"Well, this is Helge Instad," he continued, anxious to unload his tale, pointing to the man. "And his wife Anne Stine. They're archeologists from Norway. They've just discovered a Viking settlement here in the province. Told them your story." Turning to them, he explained, "Ed just finished college, he likes history." Smiling, he joked, "Thinks he knows everything."

Astounded at the unexpected revelation, I eagerly shook their hands and congratulated them. Then to show off my enthusiasm and knowledge of Nordic history, in true grandstanding fashion, I added, "Let me guess where. Cartwright, Labrador. Bjarni Herjulfesson's Markland. Right?"

Anne Stine smiled at my juvenile exuberance, but Helge Ingstad, stone-faced, answered bluntly in his stern Norwegian accent, "No! Black Duck Brook. George Decker showed it to us."

Chronicle 4

The 777 Charm

To live in a world without love is better to have died.

Legend has it that when Lazarus Edison was born at precisely midday on December 6, 1882, the earth became dark. The planet Venus deliberately transited between the earth and the sun to announce his arrival. A blessed premonition to signify the birth of a famous person endowed with magical powers and to guarantee a long, happy love life.

And for good reason.

He was the seventh son of the seventh son of the seventh son, an impossible trilogy. And as incredulous as that sounds, birth records still exist to prove there wasn't a single female in all three generations. Thus, everyone believed he had the *charm*, Ha Ha Bay's terminology for every supernatural phenomenon from psychokinesis to raising the dead. Even more potent, he had the *777 charm.* In fact, all the Edison family was *touched,* the catchall community phrase for anybody deviating from the church teachings, and that included any physically handicapped or mentally retarded person.

But religion aside, Rus, as he was nicknamed, performed paranormal events that were unexplainable, thus inadvertently demonstrating to the superstitious community that he possessed the *gift* to heal the sick, cure toothache, stop bleeding, heal sores, and a cornucopia of other maladies, and they in turn convinced him.

It all started when Rus was five years old. He was jigging fish with his father and brothers when he caught a fifty-pound squid. With an average specimen weighing one to two pounds, this was indeed a miracle, and from that point, everyone was certain he was endowed with the *power*.

A year later, he had a pet hen that laid a double egg. Not a double-yolked egg, but a complete shelled egg within an egg. This caused much consternation in the little hamlet. Soon after, he caught a *loader* codfish off the wharf. A loader was traditionally a forewarning, a good omen announcing that there would be plenty of fish and every boat would be loaded, yet there were no fish. This prompted the sanctimonious clergy to issue a warning that Rus's power was not of God but the devil, and parents were ordered to prevent their children from associating with the heathen Edison brothers.

With religion alienation, soon Ha Ha Bay began to view him as a false prophet sent to earth to corrupt godly folks, a witch doctor who sold them snake oil, a fairy to waylay travelers, an evil spirit to collect their souls, and a plethora of other derogatory fabrications. To further exacerbate their paranoia, the winter of 1882 was bitterly cold, followed by a summer of vicious storms that destroyed much fishing equipment. Even fresh berries were scarce. Soon all the misfortunes of the community were heaped on them.

But Rus didn't care. As predicted, his life was perfect, a practical bed of roses. He had the joy of his life, the rich, beautiful merchant's daughter, Rose. They had been sweethearts since childhood, inseparable, did everything together; she had stood by him during the terrible years when everyone else in the community rejected him, an unbreakable bond of love to stand the test of time. So when he reached twenty-one, having already set up a manufacturing facility to bottle his 777 charm healing medicine and a clinic to perform his *gifted* services, he proposed to her. She was ecstatic and agreed to the marriage without reservation. He was the most eligible bachelor in the community, and she would soon be wealthy like her parents. Rus was equally overjoyed. The stars had indeed provided him with a fairy-tale romance. He was madly in love with her. Their future was sealed. A famous marriage to be to be discussed throughout the annals of Ha Ha Bay's history.

Just when things couldn't get worse for the community, scurvy hit. The people got sick. All, that is, except the Edisons; they had a magic potion to cure any disease. The people being poor fishermen, Rus volunteered to cure anybody who helped him with his chores in lieu of payment. After proving his power by curing his fiancée's parents, the residents were soon cutting firewood, knitting cod traps, repairing his boats, and a host of his other responsibilities as compensation; and as promised, all were miraculously cured, even the preacher who had ostracized his family. Unselfishly saving the community consolidated his position as a divine healer, and people no longer challenged his methods. Suddenly, he was projected as a prophet of God again.

He really didn't know what had cured them; all he had done was chant an age-old family prayer and administer each patient a small portion of his 777 charm. It was an exact concoction of spruce boughs mixed with juniper berries, fungus from green trees, yeast, and pure Edison Pond water brewed in a wooden vat for two weeks until it reached an alcoholic content of 80 proof. Portions of the brew would then be simmered for fifteen minutes with freshly steamed cow's milk, as, and when, needed. It had been his great-grandmother's ancient recipe for most stomach ailments.

But one day, a young English physician, Dr. Justin Preston, appeared in the community for the first time to evaluate the heath of the people and to vaccinate children against contagious diseases, and he took a special fancy to Rose. She took an equal shine to him, enthralled by his foreign accent and cultured manners. They gelled almost as if matched by fate.

Upon hearing the news, Rus was at first skeptical; theirs was an unshakable love, built on mutual trust. But when his six trusting brothers confirmed it, he was devastated. He retaliated by interrupting the doctor's next clinic that was set up in the community elementary school and putting a 777 curse on him in front of everybody to prove his power. The doctor just laughed with exuberance, but the people were stunned; they weren't so sure. They warned the doctor that the Edison family had healed them before he arrived and had saved the people from scurvy, and they deserved some respect.

The doctor amusingly conceded Rus's milky spruce tree beer probably did cure scurvy, but it was only a stroke of luck. As for all his other miracles, they were happenstance, fake, and his magic potions *were* just snake oil.

Rose was furious when she heard the gossip that her fiancée had made her the laughingstock of the community. She stomped into Rus's home and confronted him while he was curing a sick friend.

"Idiot! How could you do something so stupid?" she began, fuming, and continued to lecture him incessantly for half an hour without giving him an opportunity to respond, as his friends, like him, watched in horror at her extreme change in character. She appeared possessed by demons.

"I'm sorry. I now regret it, sweetheart," he finally replied meekly, shocked and deeply hurt, lowering his head. "I guess it's because I loved you so much."

"What about me?" she screamed, eyes flashing, hitting the table. "Don't you care about my happiness?"

"I thought I might lose you. I wasn't thinking."

"That's because you're *touched*. A freak. You disgraced me. How could I ever marry someone so stupid?"

She flung his ring across the floor.

"I saved your life from scurvy," he ventured nostalgically. "All your family."

"Justin said you lucked out. He's a real doctor!"

"It also saved your life from blood poisoning when you cut your foot on that rusty nail when you were six."

"You have *prophetic* dreams, that's *sick!* He says you're just an insane medicine man."

"Do you love him?" he ventured nervously, hurting badly.

"With all my heart! He's intelligent, good-looking, and he's *not* a pauper like you."

"Please forgive me," he groveled. "I'll promise I'll do anything you ask."

"Good! Drown yourself!"

The superstitious community didn't want the good doctor bewitched, so they attempted to convince Rus to challenge him to a healing contest in front of a panel of the community elders. He refused. In truth, he didn't know himself how he had cured the people; it just happened as a result of his 777 charm. Instead, much to the dismay of the unbelieving community, he meekly apologized to the doctor, retracted the curse, and just gave him a list of his anomalies to explain and left the good doctor alone.

The night before, he again had had one of his prophetic dreams. It warned him that his lifelong sweetheart was gone forever without explaining why. But he believed it was probably due to his own idiotic beliefs and actions over the years. She was beautiful, smart, and rich; she really did deserve someone better.

On his next trip to Ha Ha Bay, the doctor explained to him that his giant squid at age five was just a transient Humboldt squid, and it really was just a small one; they grew up to one hundred pounds; in warmer waters, they were plentiful. The egg within an egg was due to the hen unable to lay the first egg, but he agreed it was quite uncommon. The spruce tree beer cured the scurvy because it contained vitamin C. A loader was a rare one in a million genetically defective codfish that was usually found in large schools of fish; many fishermen had caught such a fish in their lifetime. But curing Rose's blood poisoning was particularly puzzling; he could not explain it and admitted it like a true gentleman.

For the next year, Rose happily dated her beloved Justin with fanatical devotion; she worshipped him. Rus stood sadly by and patiently waited for an opportunity to present itself. He knew the doctor courted many other women and would desert her sometime, she being just his stand-in, his play toy for the few days while he visited Ha Ha Bay each month. Nonetheless, he prayed every night for God to find a practical way to help her gain Justin's love. He knew telling her the truth would make her hate him more. But none came; his prophetic dream was coming true, proof he was not deserving of such a pretty, rich girl. His charm had no affect on love. He really *was* an insane medicine man.

One stormy winter day, Justin became critically ill. His fellow doctors at the hospital determined that he had a serious infection but could not identify it with any known strain. No prescribed medicine was effective, and he was deteriorating fast. Fearing he was going to die, Justin begged Rose to consult Rus, fearing his 777 curse from a year ago was just now becoming effective.

Panicking, Rose promised Rus that if he cured him, she would break off her relationship with Justin and marry him and be his true love for all eternity. Rus said nothing and agreed to cure the doctor without any preconditions, realizing her desperation and devotion had proven Justin really was the person she loved, and he loved her too much to deny her a lifetime of happiness. He instead would use his 777 charm to provide Rose with a long happy life.

Rus willingly made the arduous eighteen-hour overland journey through the stormy night to the hospital. There he secretly had Justin swear under oath to God that if he cured him, he would marry Rose; if not, he would invoke the full force of his 777 charm and cast horrible pestilences on him for the rest of his miserable life, and his tribulations would be a picnic compared to Job's.

To the doctor, this was a peculiar conundrum, knowing Rus loved Rose whereas to him, she was just a fling. He also knew that Rus was aware of it. He had no intention of marrying her but was in no position to negotiate. He anticipated a trap but readily agreed.

All the doctors snickered and mocked as Rus performed the family ritual and recited a mantra at the doctor's bedside and gave him his *charm* medicine. As Rus acted professionally, prescribing two teaspoonfuls per day for a week, the other doctors roared with laughter. But Rus didn't care; he had to save Justin for his lifelong girlfriend.

Next day, to the amazement of the hospital staff, Justin was feeling better; within a week, he was back to excellent health. Justin's peers were astounded but still considered it mere coincidence yet an uncanny stroke of luck in lieu of his critical condition.

To stay away from Rose, Justin no longer made monthly medical visits to Ha Ha Bay. However, as months flew by, he became increasingly nervous about his secret oath and its impending curse. Without any logical explanation, he found Rose always on his mind, even when he dated other girls or in the operating room. Finally, to keep his promise and ease his conscience, after six months, he proposed, confident after such a long, silent separation Rose would reject him. But Rose had no such honorable principles. She gleefully accepted without reservations, quickly forsaking her promise to Rus.

They were married in a grand ceremony on her father's estate. Rus attended the lavish wedding long enough to see Rose happily married and to give them both his blessing and his special gift—his lucky long-life charm as a talisman to watch over them—then departed Ha Ha Bay, never to be seen again.

All his long, happy life, Justin was grateful to Rus; his marriage was indeed a gem, and in all that time, he tried unsuccessfully to figure out how Rus's mysterious charm worked. He now believed it wholeheartedly, much to the dismay of his wife.

After retiring from medicine at seventy-five, one night in 1928, as he was admiring Rus's long-life talisman, his eye caught an article in an English medical journal on how Dr. Fleming had accidently discovered that when bacteria was dropped on green tree fungus, the fungus killed it. He isolated the fungus as *Penicillium notatum*, a mold. It proved to be a miracle drug to cure infections.

It then hit Justin like bolt of lightning.

He yelled to his wife, "Rose, come here. You won't believe this!"

"What's the problem?' she asked nervously, rushing in. "Your heart's acting up, love?"

"No," he answered excitedly. "Rus was right. He did have the 777 charm."

Seeing him holding the talisman, she reprimanded, "Good grief, Justin, throw that thing away, that was fifty years ago. You still jealous? Let it go!"

"No, he didn't know it, but he discovered antibiotics," Justin continued, astounded. "The Edisons were geniuses."

"Antibiotics? What are you talking about? Charms are old wives' tales. You're a doctor for goodness sake! You're becoming senile."

"No, love," he replied solemnly. "He had green tree mold and yeast in that charm." He read her the article from the paper. "It acted as penicillin. He actually *did* save your life from that rusty nail infection. And he really *did* save my life *for you*."

She was too stunned to speak; hurtful memories flooded back. It was the first time in fifty years Rus had seriously ever entered her mind.

"For me?" she whispered finally.

"Love, there's something I have to tell you. I've kept it a secret all these years," he sniffled. "Rus made me swear to marry you in exchange for saving my life."

Tears flooded her eyes. She recalled how she had so brutally forsaken him.

But Rus would never know. Two hours after Justin and Rose were married, he had drowned himself, just as Rose had asked, not wanting to live in a world without his lifelong sweetheart.

Chronicle 5

Helping the Kriegsmarine

Adversity makes strange bedfellows.

Rumors that the Parker family of L'Anse aux Meadows provided the Germans with sensitive Allied information and their U-boats with supplies during WWII was widespread and contentious. And their instant rise in affluence soon after only exacerbated this belief by the local fishermen, who created such a commotion that it eventually reached the higher echelons of the Royal Navy, who in turn convened a court marshal to investigate the mushrooming allegations.

The panel took four years to release its classified findings and, just after Newfoundland joined Canada in 1949, revealed only that the Parkers had voluntarily initiated a secret agreement to assist the British with German submarine surveillance in the area using their offshore fishing boat in return for fuel supplies and concluded that henceforth, the Parker family were to be hailed as heroes, not traitors, and were afforded a generous pension from Britain.

But local fishermen, who closely monitored one another for safety, had observed the Parker boat rendezvousing with numerous unidentifiable ships of various sizes, including submarines on several occasions, sometimes after midnight in adverse weather conditions, and believed the pension was a cover-up in return for the Parker family keeping the incident a secret.

Two years ago, and some sixty years after the war, I investigated the rumor and was fortunate enough to locate a relative who was willing to talk. I sat down with Tim Parker, a budding writer, who was very close to his great-grandfather Calvin Parker, who asked him to write a book to tell the Parker side of the story before he died. He related a fireside chat they had just before he passed away. The following is my adaptation of that conversation.

The forties was a rebirth for many fishermen in northern Newfoundland after the depression of the dirty thirties. Plenty of work with fish prices at record highs. However, it had its drawbacks. It took a war to rejuvenate the world economy, and with war came great personal sacrifices.

L'Anse aux Meadows was in the line of fire of the enemy. It was situated at the entrance to the narrow Strait of Belle Isle, a major exit route into the Atlantic for Canadian convoys supplying Britain and a focal point for prowling German U-boat wolf packs.

Calvin Parker, living in a deep cove on the outer point, was one of the unfortunate ones. His strategically located deep-sea fishing property was confiscated for the war effort, relegating his prosperous family to his small farming shack deep into the bottom of the Bay of Islands, miles from his traditional, and lucrative, trawling grounds. His home, bunkhouses, and storerooms were requisitioned as lodging for the Canadian land forces and his docking facilities as a reprovisioning depot for Royal Navy corvettes who mined the bay, where he did a substantial portion of his fishing, to prevent German U-boats from entering.

The Parkers felt bitter. They were of German stock but were staunch Newfoundlanders. They saw both the Canadians and British as occupying forces and knew the seizure of their property was as much a result of distrust and revenge as genuine need.

In return for his service and being the only breadwinner for his wife, two daughters, and three sons—all preteens—who made up his fishing crew, Calvin was exempt from conscription. But even more humiliating, his large deep-sea fishing boat was equipped with *huff-duff,* a revolutionary radio-frequency underwater object detector, and he was ordered to report any U-boat's signals to the American air force base at Goose Bay, another occupying force.

He realized that as a German, he was a victim of circumstances and grudgingly swallowed his pride, remained quiet, and complied like an obedient puppy but inside was seething, seeing peaceful Newfoundlanders as mere pawns that supplied raw materials and dying needlessly for an alien king in a foreign war.

However, on the bright side, the Royal Navy did afford him five drums of fuel each week for his extended patrols, and diesel fuel was a precious and rare commodity during the war.

But tucked away deep into the bay, the long trips offshore to the fishing grounds or on U-boat patrols consumed valuable time that should be used for processing any fish he caught, and local fish merchants soon realized it would result in a disastrous fishing season and refused him credit. Without essential supplies, he soon became desperate.

In retaliation, he carried out no reconnaissance and did only inshore fishing. By the autumn of 1942, he had caught barely enough fish to feed his family, and survival was a daily struggle. But he had accumulated sixty drums of diesel fuel and wondered where he could illegally sell the valuable product without arousing the suspicion of the Royal Navy.

The answer presented itself in dramatic fashion just before dawn in early October while trolling for *fall fish*. The wind had picked up rapidly, a dense fogbank had rolled in, and with the swell running high, for the safety of his family, he headed for the leeward side of Big Island and entered the narrow entrance to a small sheltered, secluded cove to wait out the gale. As he rounded the point, he was surprised to see the dark silhouette of a large ship tucked snugly underneath the white overhanging cliffs.

Almost instantly, sheer pandemonium erupted all around. Several diesel engines started, the vibrations resonating off the steep rock face; ear-piercing sirens echoed, red lights began flashing, shadows were running around the deck of the mysterious boat shouting orders, outlines of objects were being lowered into the ocean, and Calvin's fishing boat was flooded with a blinding searchlight. Unable to identify each other in the semidarkness and dense fog, massive panic ensued on both boats.

Calvin ordered his family inside the cabin and quickly began to back his sixty-foot trawler out the narrow entrance when he heard a brief burst of machine gun fire and a megaphone blare "Surrender" in broken English. Then silence. He stopped and waited nervously. Soon, discernable shadows of small boats crowded with dark ghostlike figures pierced the eerie fog, circled all around him with choruses of "Halt" bombarding him from every direction.

Realizing it might be a German U-boat and he could be trapped, he took a gamble and responded hoarsely at the top of his lungs in German, "Ja wohl."

The loud, bloodcurdling metal clamor of the ship and the swirling, changing colored lights in the cold morning fog intermingled with the smell of diesel exhaust created a surreal and hypnotic atmosphere. On deck, the Parker children were surrounding their mother, hugging and crying.

Unable to fully identify the small boats, Calvin, near panic, yelled again nervously, "Willkommen," still unsure, realizing it could be a British corvette.

Putting his hands over his head, Calvin ordered his wife and five panic-stricken children to follow his example. For what seemed like an eternity, they stood apprehensively on the deck awaiting their fate. Within a few minutes, the cautious boats had circled progressively close enough for Calvin to see the features of what appeared to be a dozen or more heavily armed machine gun-toting men in several small inflatable rafts. They scrambled aboard his trawler from both sides and aft, simultaneously shouting orders.

Realizing they had captured an unarmed fishing boat, the attackers became eerily quiet. Not a word was uttered as they quickly frisked Calvin and then, with a gentler demeanor, courteously conveyed him and his family to the deck of the ship where their captain and his men were standing at attention. Calvin and his family soon realized the ship was a German submarine and they were now prisoners.

Seeing a family of fishermen, the captain ordered his submariners to put away their arms, bowed to the Parkers—as did all the others submariners—and motioned for the Parkers to lower their hands. He then yelled for the cook to bring them hot chocolate and cookies and, looking both relieved and excited, responded, "Danke schön."

"Let my family go, please," Calvin blurted angrily, with more confidence than he felt. "Take me and my boat. We're just poor fishermen."

Then out of the blue came an unbelievable request in perfect English. "You have fuel. We're low." Offering his hand in friendship, the captain switched to German. "Not poor, but we know. I'm Captain Wolfgang Steinberg. You're safe among your own people."

For some time, the Parkers stared hypnotized at the captain as he paced and stared pensively at the deck with hands behind his back, recounting his tragic voyage. Finally, as if defeated, he pleaded, "Please sell us your fuel. Now we're stranded. Our supply ship had its fuel tank punctured from a depth charge. The Kriegsmarine will pay twice the market value. In British pound sterling, of course."

Calvin was floored. Too stunned to respond. He just stood staring with his mouth open. A miracle and a curse, all in the same sentence. The other mariners remained standing at attention and smiling pleasantly as they patiently awaited his reply.

"The . . . the . . . Canadian forces' base is just four miles away," stuttered his wife emphatically, shivering from the cold, amazed at their audacity.

The captain motioned to his aide, who brought blankets and placed them snugly around her and each of the children.

"Thank you, fräulein. We know," the captain then answered kindly. "We also know that they appropriated your property without compensation. That you're now a Newfoundlander." Then sternly, but proudly, added, "And a German. Purebred. Blond even."

"We'll be shot!" exclaimed Calvin, regaining his nerve. We have the Royal Navy, the Canadian army, and the American air force here, all around us."

"In short, you're occupied now," concluded the first mate. After a brief silence in which Calvin did not respond, he added, "And they're all starving you. Yes, we know."

Seeing Calvin's youngest daughter sobbing and holding her mother, the captain touched her nose with his finger and promised, "We will not harm any of you, whatever your dad decides."

In the next while, as the conversation progressed amiably, the whole family relaxed, sipped their hot chocolate, and ate cookies, puzzled by the captain's sympathy for their pathetic situation.

"We have good fishing property," argued Calvin honestly. "The war won't last forever. We don't need help—"

"It's mined by the Anglo-Saxons," argued the captain. "And when they leave, remember, some of those drift mines will be your problem."

It never entered Calvin's mind that mines could be lost or left behind, and it irritated him that he was not adequately informed of all the dangers.

"They gave you fuel because you have the only large deep-sea fishing boat in the area, not as compensation but because they need your service. They lack reconnaissance ships," the first mate lectured affably.

"How do you know?" queried Calvin's wife.

The first mate smiled at her curiosity and answered, "The Anglo-Saxons are careless and reckless."

"You had us under surveillance, like real spies?" asked Calvin's young six-year-old daughter, Casey, inquisitively and in perfect German. "Are you going to kill us?"

"Of course not," laughed the captain. "We don't kill Germans."

"Reckless?" asked Calvin's wife, anxious to get back to the sale.

Turning to Calvin, the captain continued sternly. "They know the huff-duff on your boat is easy for us to detect. Without depth charges, you're a sitting duck. They're using you and your family as German guinea pigs. Did your Anglo-Saxon friends tell you that? The Kriegsmarine could have destroyed you months ago."

Calvin again felt the pangs of mixed emotions. His resentment for the allies resurfaced, but he said nothing.

"Your huff-duff was quite active. You knew we were in the area," the captain pressed on. "Why didn't you report us?"

"It's not my war!"

"A loyal German perhaps?" concluded the captain.

The crew applauded.

"The seas in this area can be rough—" began Calvin to warn him of the dangers of such a shallow water operation.

"That's why we're hiding here," interjected the captain. "We know. But we have weather stations all around you. We have many friends in this country."

Calvin doubted that.

Seeing Calvin's skeptical frown, the captain added, "They, like us, know your German name is not Parker."

For the next while, Calvin and the captain weighed or squabbled over the pros and cons of such a fuel deal without any significant progress. Seeing Calvin refusing, his wife angrily assailed him in German, "Sell them the damn fuel. You have sixty drums. Sixty! We don't need it. They'll take it back if you—"

The applauding crew interrupted her train of thought. The captain was surprised and elated at the huge amount.

"They will count the drums, all right," he mumbled to his wife yet somewhat irritated and puzzled at her unorthodox interference.

"And they want those empties back by Christmas," she reminded him in the same angry tone of voice.

"Need only one foggy day," nudged the captain.

Confident Calvin's wife was the boss and anxious to speed up the decision, the captain took from his pocket a large wad of five-pound notes and offered them to her. "Sorry, we don't have Newfoundland currency. Pay you £200 now, £200 will be left upon delivery."

Calvin's heart stopped. He was about to object but became frozen, unable to utter a word, as his wife quickly stepped forward and accepted the money. She knew that amount alone was four or five times the true value of the product and more money than they ever had in their lives. It would be sweet revenge for losing their property. The crew smiled with satisfaction. Or relief.

"Counterfeit!" exclaimed Calvin, realizing it may be the only option he had left at his disposal to influence his wife to return it, fully cognizant of the difficulty in convincing her.

"Quite true," smiled the captain, "but undetectable, made with plates supplied by the Royal Mint."

Convinced the deal was now sealed, he cautioned, "It's safer you stay here tonight. We know where the fuel is located. Will pick it up first opportunity. Tonight, if still foggy. On high tide."

Calvin declined staying, anxious to get his family out of harm's way and then to somehow figure out how to distance himself from the whole messy affair. Shakily, he asked they be returned to his fishing boat. The captain readily agreed, but not before purchasing their fresh catch of cod and halibut for an incredible £40 and again shaking hands with each member of his family in friendship.

Calvin now felt more trapped than ever, knowing he had sold his soul to the devil, or devils. He now had agreements with both the

British and Germans, and his direct contact was with the Americans. He hastily backed his boat slowly out the narrow channel, staring, almost bewildered, at his family standing on deck wrapped in black Nazi blankets with large red swastikas, happily talking in German, and waving excitedly to the crew of his countrymen on the U-Boat, who were joyfully waving back.

The captain cautioned, "You'll be met by friendly German U-boats on some foggy days each month or so. Keep your huff-duff active, they'll find you when the time is right. They'll be happy to purchase your catch of fresh fish and any fresh fruit and vegetable. Even local berries will suffice. I promise, your boat will be safe from all the Kriegsmarine. But stay away from your home for the next few days. It's a four-hour shallow-water operation. If we're discovered, you *know* us Germans will die with dignity."

Calvin nodded, completely defeated, and muttered sarcastically to himself, "Dignity? And I'm a traitor and a coward. I'm already dead."

Tim Parker's great-grandfather grew tired at that point but insisted on telling him the whole story of his frequent encounters with German U-boats, American carriers, British corvettes, and a host of smaller crafts over the next three years of the war, wanting the truth of his dealings to be revealed in a book to his adopted countrymen. He promised an epic tale with an ironic twist that would stun even the most ardent skeptic. But his great-grandfather died just three days later at ninety-six, and the rest of the saga died with him.

However, this much is public knowledge. After the war, the Parker's property was returned, and with the upgraded docking facilities to accommodate large ships, they purchased a 125-foot steel-hulled deep-sea trawler, which they paid for in full with British currency.

Five years later, after confederation, they sold their property at L'Anse aux Meadows to the Canadian government and moved across Island Bay to Ship Cove.

Some fifteen years later, with the Parker children now all having graduated from university, they started a shipping company, which in a few short years prospered into a major operation with two oceangoing freighters.

And as incredible as it sounds, in 1980, one of the weather stations to which the captain had referred was discovered at an elevation of 1,100 feet on Cape Chidley at the end of the Torngat Mountains on the northern tip of Labrador (now Nunavut). It was a fully automated weather station code-named Wetter-Fungerat Land-26 and was also used as a locator beacon in triangulation for ship positioning. It was still operational forty-three years later.

Tim Parker is now an author but, inexplicably, never penned a word about his ancestors. He believes his great-grandfather was a double secret agent, spying for both the British and the Germans, since the Germans knew intimate details of his family. He also speculated the Germans had moles—most likely local German Newfoundlanders—in the Royal Navy corvette detachment located on his property in L'Anse aux Meadows. He also believes the Germans had help from the Moravian missionaries in Hebron to locate the weather station and that there are other German weather stations located somewhere in northern Newfoundland, possibly on Belle Isle, as well as one in southern Greenland.

Unfortunately, Tim Parker has been ostracized by all the Parker descendants for disclosing this story to me.

Chronicle 6

A Halloween to Remember

A real jack-o'-lantern.

Newfoundland in 1919 had a high percentage of the people of Celtic descent that fled Ireland during the potato famine of the 1840s, and each October 31, the Celtic All Hollows'een, or New Year's Eve, brought back memories of their ancient customs and stories of their heritage from those days back in dear old Erin. And as a result, the adults were just as enthusiastic about donning costumes and going trick-or-treating as the children, except they justified it by arguing that even though it was a pagan tradition, they saw it as a tool to keep their ancestral tradition alive, and they only pretended to worship their lord of the dead, Samhain.

The Protestants clergy, who represented the English descendants, however, urged their congregation's children not to participate in these heathen rituals, it having originated with the cannibalistic Druids, who could still call forth satanic spirits from oak trees to perform ghoulish acts on anybody in the community partaking in such unholy practices.

Nineteen nineteen was an especially dangerous year. WWI had just claimed ten million lives, and now, the pale horseman of the apocalypse had appeared and was casting its evil deeds worldwide in the guise of a flu pandemic that began in Spain and was poised to wipe out the world. Mankind was paying dearly for its carnal nature. And this was the prophetic year in which the Lord was to send forth a host of heavenly angels out of the firmament to cleanse such wicked pagan rituals.

As in every year before, the Protestant clergy for weeks had fervently preached to their youth to wait another five days for Bonfire Night, the day Guy Fawkes tried to blow up parliament, and celebrate their own heritage. This would be righteous and pleasing in God's sight and bring an abundance of blessings. But trying to convince rambunctious children, who couldn't care less about religion, to forgo two parties within a week was a pipe dream.

Indeed, secretly, everybody appreciated the reprieve from the drudgery of a long summer of fishing and farming and was eager to participate. It had been a bountiful season, and whether it be Samhain, Beltane, or the Druid's Muck Olla himself, it was a reason to celebrate. The houses were all stacked with goodies: berries, apples, nuts, and lots of baked goods, especially hot cross buns. A bitter cold winter loomed ahead.

And as in previous years, the Catholics found the Protestants' threat amusing. Not wanting to be outclassed, they retaliated by facetiously offering up a dire warning of their own concoction. They would send a multitude of fairies, leprechauns, witches, banshees, plus all the dead spirits of the community to fight the host of angels.

The ludicrous news spread like wildfire, and the contest soon became the joke of the community, lifting everyone's spirits, and in the end, religion was forgotten; Halloween Night found everyone from toddlers to great-grandparents of all religions blended together and marching single file down the narrow winding path, dressed in a cornucopia of ridiculous, macabre costumes, carrying hollowed-out painted-faced turnips with candles inside, a ghoulish parade of joyful living spirits with lanterns to light their way between the widely spaced houses. Their leaders carrying skeletons on crosses and skulls on stakes and performing bizarre body motions to scare away any evil demons and ghosts that may be stalking them. All making bloodcurdling noises.

It was an unusually calm, crisp autumn night with a brilliant dancing aurora borealis, millions of twinkling stars, and a full harvest moon illuminating the land, when there mysteriously emerged from the northeast a steady pulsing sound like a steamship's engine. Hundreds of heads turned skyward to view, just a few hundred feet above the ground, a huge black object with dozens of multicolored flashing lights in a perfect straight line. First, the merry partiers thought it might be one of the newfangled flying objects some soldiers returning from the war had talked about called aeroplanes. But this object was gargantuan, at least a thousand feet long. It appeared scarcely moving and lingering, as if searching for something. It suddenly turned and headed directly for them. The viewers became nervous. Maybe it was a UFO from Mars. There were occasional bursts of fire being emitted from the object's tail, and it trailed smoke far behind. Or was it a mythical dragon? The celebrants were superstitious, but UFOs and dragons were difficult pills to swallow. Nonetheless, the group was concerned.

As it slowly approached, strange, melodious, blissful music like a heavenly choir could be heard above the rhythmic thumping of the beast. Several bright lights then flooded the marchers. The music became louder. Some smaller creatures floating just below the larger mother creature seemed to be harkening to them.

Then the Protestant clergy's prediction hit everyone like a bolt of lightning from heaven, literally. The music was the Lord's host coming to collect his righteous servants. The people became frozen, mesmerized.

This was it! There could no longer be any doubt. The prophecies were indeed true. Armageddon was nigh, the end time the Bible had forewarned. The second coming of Christ had literary sneaked upon them like a thief in the night, and they were all caught worshipping a pagan god. Salvation was lost!

The Halloweeners became stricken; sheer panic replaced amazement.

The Protestants silently prayed. Their clergy had been correct. The adult females, who were not drunk, or believing they were hallucinating, were crying.

The Catholics reverently crossed themselves, utterly confused. Why had the Protestants won? If so, who were the contestants? There was no fighting. Why wasn't their multitude of fairies, leprechauns, witches, banshees, and all those dead spirits their priest promised protecting them? Anxiety increased.

Hundreds of darker objects could be hazily distinguished surrounded by what appeared to be bright halos. But weren't angels supposed to be white? Or were they devils? No! It then became blatantly obvious. The black figures were angels looking out the windows of the promised eternal city of Jerusalem that was floating down from heaven. They were mortified at their situation. This was supposed to be a glorious event; instead they were trapped in satanic costumes worshipping the devil. "No man knoweth the hour," they recalled forlornly.

The heavenly city inched menacingly closer. The music abruptly stopped. The Halloween procession became deathly quiet, still stalled in their tracks, transfixed skyward. Cows and sheep could be heard softly mooing and baaing a celestial greeting. Dogs began to howl as if trumpeting the king's arrival. The invading armada turned and eerily silhouetted itself against the ever-changing colored aurora borealis and the starry background, displaying its gigantic appearance more ominously. From this angle, it appeared to be a sinister fire-breathing dragon again.

On and on it crept; larger and larger it loomed overhead until it mysteriously blacked out the moon, casting its deathly shadow directly over its target, the pagan Halloweeners below. The creature's pulsing sound stopped briefly as it caught its breath. The sacred music resumed. Louder this time. Now it resonated more like a church choir of the heavenly host again.

The watchers were too hypnotized to move, obediently awaiting their fate like lambs at a slaughter as closer and closer their impending doom approached from above.

Then miraculously, a church bell rang out, pealing their death knell, their final opportunity for sinners to come and repent before the final assault. The marchers dropped everything, peeling of their pagan costumes as they bolted for their respective churches. Soon praises were echoing across the waters of the bay and reverberating of the cliffs. The Catholic priest gave communions and confessions en masse. The priest heard how some of its members practiced all the seven deadly sins and broke all the Ten Commandments daily, in front of the whole congregation, as they insisted on openly confessing their sins, all in record time, hoping a merciful God would grant them some degree of leniency.

Families were rapidly assembled. Nine o'clock found a solemn community, the rich and the poor, the meek and the powerful, the old and the young, the good and the bad, the sober and the drunk, the master and the slave, all sitting patiently in their church pews, silently holding hands, heads bowed, waiting for their judgment, hoping for forgiveness and rapture, but fearing damnation and burning in everlasting hell.

Meanwhile, at the wireless operating station near St. Anthony, the Morse code operator had just received the following transmission:

Cape Bauld Station

The Royal Navy-R34 dirigible will pass over your beacon on October 31 at approximately 2100 hours. Stop. It will descend to 500 feet to take bearing. Stop. Relay message to Roosevelt Field, Mineola, New York, upon observation. Stop. Advise them estimated time of arrival at New York is now Nov 2, 1919. Stop. Send confirmation. Stop.

Royal Navy HQ

Chronicle 7

Gifts of the Magi

Only a fine line separates genius from insanity.

Eking out a subsistence living on the windswept coast of northern Newfoundland was precarious at best and often catastrophic. Its residents were a rugged, hardworking, resilient people that had settled the unforgiving land and had taken the worst nature could throw at them. But 1913 was particularly bleak. All summer, it was stormy and frigid, the bay remained full of arctic ice preventing fishing, and by August, the cod fishery had failed disastrously. Not even enough for food, much less for sale. Thus people had no money to buy staples like flour, sugar, or tea. The small gardens produced few vegetables due to the late planting, the cold, and the lack of fish as fertilizer. The few stunted vegetables that survived were rendered inedible by worms or disease.

In the fall, migratory birds, which residents traditionally bottled as a source of protein for the frigid winters, had failed to return. Even worse, the numerous species of wild berries, which normally flourished in abundance on the barren boggy land, had shriveled and died before maturing, and berries were the only fruits fishermen had in their diets during the long winter. To add insult to injury, several of the children had severe breathing problems, probably consumption. The future loomed apocalyptic.

As was customary, the people moved away from the coastline of Ha Ha Bay in the fall to live in winter cabins at the bottom of Pistolet Bay, where firewood was readily available, and to take advantage of the forested areas as shelter from the vicious winds and snowstorms. It was also closer to their animal traplines, their meager winter source of revenue. But this year, after a month, the animals were scarce, even for food, and by December, starvation stared them in the face.

The twenty destitute families, whose cabins were all within a mile of each other, met on the frozen bay ice at the mouth of Western Brook on December 15 to devise a survival plan and ration their few remaining provisions. Conditions were desperate. No store-bought goods remained. All food was local: arctic char, smelts, a few rabbits, and one small black bear. Barely enough to feed them until Christmas. Defeated, the hundred souls knelt and prayed, pleading to God to send a miracle.

Just then, Loony Larry Tucker with his dog team came racing toward them at full speed across the frozen bay, screaming at the top of his lungs.

Larry was an anomaly. He had mysteriously appeared in Ha Ha Bay ten years earlier begging for a fishing job. Being fanatically antireligious and dramatically eccentric, he was considered retarded, and everyone refused to hire him except Clayton Butt. Since then, he had lived like a hermit, far from everyone, all year round, in the bottom of Pistolet Bay on the seashore near Loon Creek; thus, he came to be called Loony Larry. He returned to Ha Ha Bay in the summer each year to fish with Clayton and nobody else. Where he came from, or why, was an oft-discussed mystery. He appeared paranoid of guns but was undoubtedly the area's best fisherman and a trapper who could sniff out wild animals. He was well dressed, lived in a large orderly cabin, and always had plenty of food.

Everyone nervously stood up. Loony Larry had a strict code of disassociation with them after the fishing season ended. It was an ominous sign. What else could go wrong? Should they run? At first, they just stared speechless, not knowing if the ice were collapsing beneath them or the sky was falling in.

Upon Loony Larry reaching them, they were stunned to see two large caribou on his sled.

"There were thousands of them," Larry boasted, panting, overexcited, and wondering why nobody was questioning his load. "I was just cutting firewood when they came right up to me, touched their nose on my shoulder, and said, 'Kill me.' So I killed two with my axe. Tame as bloody cows."

The group stared even more, dumbfounded, still desperately trying to rationalize what they were seeing and hearing.

Hundreds? They knew Larry was a little touched and that caribou couldn't talk, but how did he kill two animals without a gun in an area where wild caribou seldom frequented? Though considered retarded, Larry was a very successful and knowledgeable person, surprisingly crafty.

"Manna from heaven," Mary Jane Butt finally offered, crossing herself. But most listeners thought differently, bullshit from weird Larry. The religious ones shuddered at the sight of him, no doubt a bad omen from the devil, probably come to collect their souls. Nonetheless, reality dictated he did have two carcasses on his sled.

"There's no caribou here, Larry," whispered Rod Taylor halfheartedly, not wanting to be ridiculed as dense, knowing the proof in front of him was undeniable.

"'Tis too, my son. Over there on Bakeapple Marsh. Seen four or five Indians too. Bloody Beothuks I think."

Everyone relaxed and laughed, knowing the Beothuks had been extinct for nearly a hundred years.

"What did the Indians look like?" asked Aunt Polly Butt, scared it might be true. Her father had told her bedtime stories about how he had fought them in the same area of Pistolet Bay where Larry now lived; it had been their ancestral hunting and fishing grounds.

"I told you. They were dressed in caribou skins and had spears."

Everyone became deadly serious. For a time, there was a tense quiet as that remote possibility was digested.

"Jesus, Larry, be serious. You're fuckin' scaring everybody," her husband, Clayton, nervously chastised, fearing they might now have to fight Indians as well as the cold, starvation, and disease.

"The Indians were friendly though. But they drove the caribou away, so I couldn't kill any more," he elucidated angrily. "They shouted at me in some queer, savage language."

The group wasn't really sure whether Larry had gone completely insane or whether they were dreaming. Not knowing what to do, Rod offered questioningly, "Share them up I suppose?"

Having divided up the animals, the men, with Larry's persuasion, decided to go hunting next day to kill enough for the winter. The temperature was now sufficiently cold for the meat to stay permanently frozen until March. But nobody expected to find any more caribou, suspecting Larry had just happened upon two caribou trapped in the deep snow. Finding more was remote and wishful thinking. However, Larry was adamant, warning them to tell absolutely nobody about it so they could keep all the caribou for themselves.

Half of the men would stay behind to guard the women in case Loony Larry's Indian story was true, and Clayton Butt would take his three sick grandchildren to the Grenfell Hospital at St. Anthony, now that Dr. Grenfell was rumored to be back from a trip to Europe.

Dr. Grenfell, a British surgeon of the benevolent Royal National Mission to Deep Sea Fishermen, had been sent to the coast in 1892, some twenty years earlier, to help the fishermen of northern Newfoundland and Labrador. More than a doctor, he was a lecturer, social worker, manager, and magistrate who held court with the power of life and death over the area's poverty-stricken illiterate people. He acted as a multidenominational preacher and held religious services to civilize a people who had lived generations without law and order. He also traveled widely in Europe and America to raise funds for an orphanage, a hospital, schools, and docking facilities. He worked tirelessly to bring the people into the twentieth century. With all his abilities, he was soon elevated to the status of demigod.

But with the respect generated by his work, his inflated ego soon enabled him to take advantage of his charitable society's position. His unlimited power corrupted him, and he became a tyrant, abusing the same people who worshipped him and, some say, a notorious womanizer. He charged people excessively for his service, taking payment from their meager earnings in fish, firewood, or labor. He thus started his own organization and began to erect a monument to himself, and in turn, the people worked for him for starvation wages, sometimes an apple a day, thus becoming his building blocks to immortality.

For the next few days, it was too stormy to go outside, but December 20 dawned crisp and sunny, and by six o'clock, seven dog teams were assembled in a circle on the bay as the men discussed and drafted a credible plan into the fresh snow on the best strategy to surround Backeapple Marsh to entrap the wild caribou. After a few initial arguments, they agreed with Loony Larry, but the whole setup felt stupid to them, especially since he insisted on leading the group, and he had taken them on wild-goose chases before. But then again, in all fairness, he had always seemed to have been successful in his ridiculous escapades.

By now, Clayton Butt had already left for the hospital in St. Anthony with the children to visit Dr. Grenfell.

The ten-mile winding journey through the bushes surrounding the marsh produced a pleasant surprise. They happened to find a large field of frozen squash berries, enough for the winter. Picking a few gallons for Christmas pies, they pressed on to find the caribou herd.

Four grueling hours later, as the seven teams converged on the small marsh from separate directions, there was utter astonishment. They stopped and stared wide-eyed in disbelief. In the centre were at least a hundred caribou, casually feeding, oblivious to their approach. Jubilant, they hand signaled one another, corralled their dog teams in the dense perimeter forest, and cautiously approached the animals with their guns ready as not to panic them, careful to give the large herd a clear way out should their gunshots stampede them after Larry gave the signal.

But Loony Larry refused to give any signal, and to their incredulity, the animals walked right up to meet them. The animals even nosed them as Larry had predicted. The seven men felt the situation positively bizarre as they stood amid a herd of tame caribou as Loony Larry selected which ones to kill while these same animals were licking salt off their faces. For a time, they happily patted and played with the animals.

Being friendly and as gentle as little lambs, they were no longer sure if they could harm them. They sensed that something was drastically strange with such an unnatural scenario but could not come up with a logical explanation. For ten minutes, a lively debate ensued if they should kill them. But the awe soon dissipated, and the argument came to an abrupt decision when Loony Larry jolted them back to reality.

"I'm supposed to be the fucking crazy one. We're starving, and you arseholes are arguing over hurting them. For Christ's sake, they're your food for the winter."

Humiliated by their folly, Rod raised his gun. Larry grabbed it and snapped, "Dummy! You'll alert the savages. Why waste bullets? I told you, they won't run away. I'll kill them with my bloody axe."

Rod started go fetch his axe, but Larry again grabbed him, this time shaking him angrily. "No! I'm in charge, I'll do all the killings. All! Understand? I have my axe here. We need to kill only seven big bucks."

An hour later, seven animals were dead, skinned, quartered, and lashed unto sleds. The dogs were fed with the surplus, and the homeward journey began.

Suddenly there appeared from the forest a caribou-clad man, bellowing and waving a spear in his hand, riding on a sled pulled by four caribou, galloping straight for them.

"That's the fucking Indians," yelled Larry. "Them Beothuks again." He grabbed Rod's gun and fired into the air to warn the others.

The Indian fell flat onto his sled as the team of caribou stopped, made a quick U-turn, and hastily retreated.

"You got the Beothuk," hollered Rod with pride.

"I didn't shoot at the Ind—"

"He's looked more like Santa Claus," interrupted Rod, now scared. "Let's go. We're not allowed to kill savages anymore." However, secretly he actually believed it to be Santa Claus but was too embarrassed to repeat it.

Whips were cracked, and in record time, the seven dogsleds were mushing homeward at full speed with their precious cargo.

Back at home, the hungry people soon learned the more undesirable details of the bountiful hunt, and some were now worried about retaliation for shooting the Indian, but all were nonetheless happy they now had nine caribou, enough meat for the winter for everyone. And berries. Things were looking up.

Clayton was relieved, as much for himself as the children, after two days of sleeping on a cold hard floor in the hospital annex as he waited for them to be examined and treated in the hospital ward. The bad news was the children were undernourished and somewhat anemic, but the good news was it could be corrected with meat, fruit, and vitamins. However, he was anxious and confused about another issue. Each day, he heard grumblings from the medical staff about someone slaughtering Dr. Grenfell's animals. He wondered who would kill such a good doctor's work dogs, his only mode of transportation in winter. Now, as he was leaving, he heard someone say that two members of the Newfoundland Rangers had been sent out to Pistolet Bay to find the killers of nine of Dr. Grenfell's animals and the person who had shot at one of their handlers. He wondered why Dr. Grenfell needed nine work dogs and who would be mean enough to shoot their handler.

As he tucked the children snugly into his sled box and covered them, he met an old friend who explained the bizarre situation to him. Clayton felt as if he had been struck by a mallet. In his eighty-five years, he had never heard such an unbelievable story! This was indeed going to be a disastrous year for all. Without wasting another minute, he raced back to Pistolet Bay, hoping to arrive in time to save his family and friends. He felt since he had only few years left, he would take full responsibility and spend those last years in jail.

Arriving back in Pistolet Bay, Clayton was met with sheer disbelief. The two rangers were at the cabin of his oldest son, John, sitting at the table, wolfing down his wife's delicious roasted caribou as they expounded on the severe repercussions to the poachers when caught. His own son was naively explaining exactly how Loony Larry had selected and killed the tame caribou from a herd of hundreds and had no idea the rangers were fully aware of what they were eating. Even admitting that Larry had shot at a savage Beothuk. All now seemed lost; Clayton knew he could not now claim responsibility himself.

Clayton quickly broke up the meal and apologized to the rangers with the excuse the children had a contagious disease and an emergency meeting had to be called immediately to prevent its spread, ordering his son to go summon the others.

Within an hour, the edgy, somber twenty families had all assembled in the crisp night air in bright moonlight in front of Clayton's cabin, surrounded by glowing torches. They could see Clayton was troubled as he stood on his sled and spoke.

"The children are fine," he began unenthusiastically as all made a sigh of relief. "But we have a big problem."

Loony Larry cringed; he knew Clayton had been in St. Anthony, heard what had happened, and that someone had talked.

"Those animals we killed were not caribou. And the person Larry shot at wasn't an Indian."

It became noisy as everybody stirred in the dry squeaky snow and began to talk, utterly confused at the remarks. They figured the old man was becoming senile. They had seen caribou before.

Clayton paused to let the commotion die down and continued. "The nine animals were reindeer, and the reindeer sleigh driver was Sammi Clas, a Laplander—"

Laughter erupted from the adults, now sure Clayton was now as loony as Larry. A chorus of jeers followed.

"Santa Claus and his reindeer are not due for another week," mocked Rod, taking a drink of moonshine. "Wait! No, look! Here he is now," pointing to a shooting star.

"Well, Jesus, Mary, and Joseph!" exclaimed Mary Jane, crossing herself. "My own husband's gone batty."

All the children began screaming and talking over each other, bombarding him with questions and heaping abuse from all angles.

"You shot Santa Claus?'

"You killed all nine of Santa's reindeer?"

"We ate Rudolph the red-nosed reindeer?"

"We'll get no presents ever again?"

Seeing the meeting rapidly deteriorating, Loony Larry jumped upon the sled beside Clayton and yelled angrily, "Shut the hell up and listen to your elder. He got you this far. Show some bloody respect."

The offensive remark from the retard riled the scoffers, but the heckling stopped abruptly, and soon the only sound breaking the eerie silence was the crackling of the northern lights.

Clayton continued. "Dr. Grenfell imported a herd of 1,200 reindeer from Norway and five Lapland herders to teach local people how to tend them like cattle. They live and eat outdoors, winter and summer, no cutting grass or stables, like for cows. They can act like dogs to pull our sleds, you can use them for food, milk, and even use their hides for clothes. They can—"

"And I told the rangers exactly who killed them and how we each took our share," John interrupted apologetically, anxious to get his infraction out in the open.

The crowd was now riled as well as shocked. All eyes now turned to their senile elder to provide a solution.

"We'll all go to the pen," added John, horrifying them further.

"I wanted to take the blame, but John had already told the rangers everything—" Clayton pressed on.

Again a commotion erupted, attacking John for his stupidity.

Once more, Loony Larry jumped upon the sled and confronted them. "I may be loony, but you people are all bloody chicken." Regaining silence, he continued. "All you sniveling cowards are safe. Remember, I killed all the reindeer, and I'll take all the blame. If asked, just say 'Retarded Larry did it.'"

"They'll hang you," whispered Mary Jane, feeling sorry for him.

"No! They'll send me to the loony bin, that's all. Now go home and look after your families. They'll be here for me tomorrow." As he began to walk away, he warned, "This time keep your bloody traps shut, except 'Loony Larry did it,' if asked. Understand?"

All nodded.

Larry headed for his cabin five miles distant as the crowd dissipated like defeated ghosts all pondering their fate.

It was Christmas Eve. The stinky fishing shed used as a makeshift courtroom was full to overflowing, and all Larry's friends sat quietly dreading his fate, knowing the judge, Dr. Grenfell, was not a forgiving person.

"Judge Grenfell presiding," yelled the acting sheriff, who was also Dr. Grenfell's ship's captain, as soon as the previous case was completed.

"Mr. Larry Tucker vs. the Crown. Destruction of Crown property in the form . . ."

After the charges were speedily read in a layman's abbreviated format and the rangers—the acting Crown prosecutors—presented their case, Loony Larry took the stand in his own defense and pleaded not guilty by reason of insanity. Then disregarding his own plight, he calmly explained the cause of people's poverty was not just due to lack of natural resources, but mostly ignorance and antiquated beliefs, even detailing the various hardships and sickness over the years that could have been easily avoided. Larry's unorthodox court finesse and expert oration confused the illiterate fisherman. He even justified his defense by reading quotes from the Bible on how Jesus fed the four thousand. You could hear a pin drop. Nobody could ever have imagined Loony Larry could read. Dr. Grenfell, unusually quiet and pensive, wholeheartedly agreed with him but remained silent, occasionally nodding his approval. Larry continued unabated to a spellbound audience for twenty minutes before the doctor-judge cut the trial short.

"Why do they call you loony, Mr. Tucker?"

"Because I'm crazy, Your Honor."

"Who told you that? A crazy person doesn't know he's crazy."

Larry did not answer.

"Did you shoot at Sammi Clas?" Mr. Tucker.

"I don't own a gun, sir. But I took Rod's and fired into the air to scare him off.

"Why?"

"I thought the others might at shoot him."

"Did you?"

"Yes, sir, he ran away. I would never hurt anybody, not even a Beothuk."

"Beothuk, Mr. Tucker? Is it possible that you already knew about the reindeer and planned the killings as an act of mercy to save your people from starvation and are now taking the blame for them? Explain why you were the only person to kill an animal?"

Loony Larry's friends held their breath in nervous anticipation. They too had wondered about that. Something was indeed fishy.

"I'm the only one to blame, sir, they *did* look like caribou. But it is true some of my friend's children would have died of hunger. You see, I'm just a retard, Your Honor."

The judge pondered for some time as the court became increasingly nervous and remained eerily silent. He then smiled.

"Do you know what reindeer looks like now?"

"Oh yes, Your Honor. They have bigger horns than caribou, and tonight they will pull Santa Claus's sleigh."

Some snickered. Others bowed their heads in despair, knowing Larry would be sent to a mental asylum.

"Will you kill any more, Mr. Tucker?"

"Oh, no, Your Honor. I only killed nine. All bucks. Old ones. Barely enough for the winter.

To everyone's surprise, the no-nonsense Dr. Grenfell shook his head and roared with laughter. "Larry, it is postulated only a fine line separates genius from insanity. We're both smart enough to know which side of that line you're on, don't we?"

Larry kept his head lowered as not to make eye contact with him and didn't answer.

Tapping his gavel joyfully on the desk, the judge stated, "However, justice must be executed. This court rejects your plea of guilty by reason of insanity, Mr. Tucker."

There was a prolonged pause.

The room became a somber place. Silent tears escaped the eyes of a few of the hardened fishermen who were no strangers to adversity. Women began to cry softly. Loony Larry bowed reverently to the judge, stepped forward, and held out his hands for the rangers to handcuff him.

"And finds you innocent. This case is now closed. You're free to go, Mr. Tucker."

On Christmas Day, instead of individual family dinners, a grand thanksgiving feast was held at Pistolet Bay in Loony Larry's honor at his very own cabin. It was the first time in ten years that Larry did not eat alone at Christmas. He had finally been accepted by his friends.

"Let's thank our Larry, he saved all our lives from starvation and from a hanging," ordered a relieved and thankful Clayton, dropping the word *loony*, standing up at the table and raising his glass of moonshine as a toast.

"No! Say grace. 'Twas the gifts of the magi," preached Mary Jane. "The good Lord fed us," she said, folding her hands and looking reverently toward heaven.

"He does work in mysterious ways," Rod chimed in.

"Good Lord? Magi? My arse," scoffed Larry chewing a mouthful of reindeer. "Forget your damn religion. Start believing in yourselves. Thank the good doctor for his kindness instead."

Mary Jane cringed at the unholy suggestion and crossed herself.

Clayton gave a sly smile and mused, *And Larry's the one who works in mysterious ways?*

Chronicle 8

The Truth about the Viking Settlement at L'Anse aux Meadows

History is what people write, the past is what happened;
the dollar trumps the facts.

Any resident of Ha Ha Bay over seventy will tell you the popular romanticized version of the discovery of the Viking settlement at L'Anse aux Meadows is a cleverly concocted deception and, in honest, open Newfie tradition, will unequivocally enlighten you to this fact: history is what people write, the past is what happened; the dollar trumps the facts.

No Viking landed there!

The biggest misconception is that Helge Ingstad and Anne Stine discovered the site. The *hummocks* or *knolls,* as the locals called them, on Black Duck Brook were common knowledge. Nearly every person in northern Newfoundland and southern Labrador knew the mounds existed before these archeologists were even born. In fact, the mounds they rediscovered were used by the Beothuks, the Micmacs, Basque whalers, French fishermen—who named it L'Anse aux Méduses (Jellyfish Cove)—and fishermen from a dozen other nations. I myself knew of the hummocks before the archeologists and had picked bakeapples there.

Helge Ingstad and his wife, Anne Stine, the real archeologist, searching around the shores of Pistolet Bay for the site of which they knew a Mr. Munn had calculated fifty years earlier as the most likely landing area of the Norsemen, lucked out. In fact, there is an age-old legend that the exact Viking site is at Milan Arm in that bay. This chronicle was relayed to the archeologists by one of Ha Ha Bay's oldest and most respected residents, Walter Taylor. But realizing he was not being taken serious, Walter directed them to see his good friend George Decker at L'Anse aux Meadows to check out the Indian hummocks at Black Duck Brook.

In the ensuing years, as the ubiquitous European artifacts in the hummocks were unearthed, interest in the archeological site progressed, and enthusiasm mounted proportionately as the media hyped the impending discovery until eventually, facts were juxtapositioned with fiction to match the preprogrammed Norse model, and the site became a self-fulfilling prophesy.

But there is an old Indian tale that was told to the first settlers of Ha Ha Bay by Louis Beaufield, a member of a Micmac tribe that lived in the bottom of Pistolet Bay that merits attention. Louis was the illegitimate son of a Micmac woman and a French doctor, Voltaire Beaufield, who frequented the area when it was part of the French shore. It contends that the mounds at L'Anse aux Meadows were built by Joao Vas Corte-Real, a Portuguese adventurer, and his sons, Miguel and Gaspar, about 1472, during an epic voyage with a fleet of many ships sponsored by the king of Portugal in conjunction with the king of Denmark, Christian I. The ragtag group, with its lethal concoction of scalawag captains: Didrik Pining, a nobleman and privateer from Norway, John Scolvus, a fearless legendary mariner from Germany, and Hans Pothorst, a Danish privateer "governed only by loot." They set out from Norway and headed westward to Iceland, then on to Greenland. Some twenty-six years before Giovanni Caboto's epic landing at Bonavista in Terra Nova.

But as the summertime daylight waned and the weather cooled, the restless adventurers turned and headed farther south along a "rugged, rocky coast" (named Lavrador by Corte-Real's countryman, Joao Fernandes Lavrador, a quarter century later in 1498) and then along a "well-treed flat area" until they came to a narrow strait (Strait of Belle Isle). They chronicled having encountered hostile natives and having to flee for their lives at three separate locations.

They finally stopped in "a flat-meadowed area on the island side of the narrow strait" and took on supplies and then continued exploring as far south as present-day New England. There they recorded having encountered numerous friendly native tribes and "endless lush flora and fauna" unknown in the old country. Their desire to stay and accurately document their findings was dashed when early autumn storms forced their departure.

On their homeward voyage, recognizing L'Anse aux Meadow's strategic location in the narrow strait, Joao and his sons built "crude earthen shelters" and made it a staging point for future exploratory venture. There they stockpiled some of their nonperishable provisions that had been collected from further south, including fruit and nuts, before continuing homeward. Following the contours of the island, twelve days later they also stopped in "a fine harbor with steep walls and a narrow entrance" that Joao named after himself, Sao Joao (St. John's.) Sao Joao was later duly recorded as such on a Portuguese map by Pedro Reinel in 1519.

Returning to Portugal in 1474, as a reward for discovering the New World, Joao was given a generous pension and an admiralship of Terceira Island in the Azures by the grateful Spanish king. Joao named his newfound land Terra Nova do Bacalhau (New Land of Codfish). He also reported the narrow strait was a funneling point for numerous species of whales heading north during summer for feeding. His findings would later touch off wars among the European nations for cod, as well as a race for an even more precious commodity, whale oil.

Christian I of Denmark promoted Didrik Pining to nobleman and made him governor of Iceland. Hans Pothurst continued his adventures for the king until his scalawags mutinied for a share of the spoils, and he "met a miserable death on the gallows." John Scoves continued his adventuresome seamanship and disappeared into the North Atlantic.

Joao, satisfied with his discovery, retired to govern his island. But he was quarrelsome with his uneducated serfs and soon realized he did not possess the patience for a governor; exploration was in his blood. Furthermore, his young and restless sons were unceasingly pestering him to return to seafaring. Secretly, with his newfound fame and riches, he outfitted several ships and headed out again, this time without his impatient, uncontrollable sons, back to the New World.

He never returned. Twenty years later, Portugal officially considered him lost.

Miguel, having matured in his father's absence, had assumed governorship of his father's domain, but his father's enemies were propositioning the king for his property. Miguel knew his father's mentality best and speculated he was not dead, so handing over his admiralty to his younger brother Gaspar, he sailed away into the unknown with the king's blessing of three new ships to search for gold, the glory of God, and Cathay. But secretly, it was to solve his father's disappearance.

Not finding him at their home base at L'Anse aux Meadows, he continued further down the coast than they had gone on the first voyage, meticulously searching every bay and cove. He met many natives who had seen "white ghost ships" heading ever further south. All summer long, with a near mutinous crew, he tenaciously pressed deeper south.

In late August, at a sheltered river, he happened upon his father's ships anchored near a large seaside Indian village with European-style housing. He was astounded to find his father and crew all living happily, having made friends with the local tribe, the Algonquian Indians, and all had taken wives. His father, who by now had two wives and three more sons, joyously explained that because of the overabundance of food, the open and carefree lifestyle, and the warm climate—and just as likely, abundance of available young females—they had all opted to stay.

Like his father, it only took a few months for the restless young Miguel to appreciate the splendor and lushness of the new country with its open and unrestricted lifestyle. The chief, impressed at such a brave young man being a great captain with three ships, gave him his youngest daughter as a gift to take back to Portugal. But Miguel fell in love with the beautiful maiden immediately and, being religious, married her within a month. This prompted him to stay for the winter to write a more detailed log of his travels for the king. But next spring, the peaceful Algonquian chief died of measles, leaving him obligatory chief of the tribe, thus compelling him to remain and make it his home as well.

In 1501, when none of his father's or his brother's ships failed to return, Gaspar Corte-Real considered it most unusual that six ships would so mysteriously disappear and set out to search for them.

Arriving again at L'Anse aux Meadows, he found evidence that his brother had been there but could not decide which direction to sail from there. Believing his kin may have tried to find the northwest passage to Cathay, he sailed up the coast of Lavrador, but after months of fruitless searching even the smallest coves and being confronted by ever-increasing ice floes and aggressive natives, he headed back to his base in L'Anse aux Meadows.

There he found his shelters occupied by Beothuk Indians. Being too late in the year for exploration further south and having no gold to take back to his king, he captured fifty-seven of them and took them back to Portugal to be sold as slaves. Thus, unknowingly initiating the first step in the extermination of the Beothuk people.

The next year, Gaspar set out again, taking the same route across the Atlantic, but fierce nor'easterly gales drove him far off course, and he landed on a small island he named Isle do Bacalhau (Codfish Island). But he knew it was not the land his father named *Terra Nova do Bacalhau.* He took on freshwater and some birds for food and forged on until he found L'Anse aux Meadows. There, after a month stopover to repair his storm-ravaged ships and take on more provisions, he headed south. Two months later and a thousand miles further south, he found the missing ships of his father and brother.

After learning the unusual circumstances, his brother Miguel, now a revered Algonquian chief, greeted him with a grand week-long family reunion feast that included all the luxuries the New World could offer. Impressed, Gaspar, like his relatives before him, first decided to stay for just one winter, but the unlimited freedom soon enveloped him as well until he too decided not to return.

Years later, the king of Portugal considered Gasper Corte-Real lost to the stormy North Atlantic as well.

In 1674, Quakers from England, settling near the shore of the Taunton River near Berkeley, Massachusetts, noticed the friendly Indians in that area were paler than other natives they had encountered and possessed strikingly familiar European features. When questioned, the natives explained their "ancient chiefs" had also come across the sea in "big white ghost ships" and then directed them to a large rock submerged in the river (Dighton Rock, now moved to a state park) with numerous native Indian petroglyphs and inscriptions. One of these petroglyphs displayed the Portuguese coat of arms of Miguel Corte-Real with the inscriptions that was translated to read, "Miguel Cortereal by will of God, here Chief of the Indians, 1511."

Two centuries later in 1847, a professor at the local university also identified a remarkable accurate depiction of the coast of Strait of Belle Isle with a marker indicating the Corte-Real's rendezvous point at L'Anse aux Meadows, just as Louis Beaufield's legend had indicated.

It was rumored that for more than ten years after the discovery, Anne Stine herself half-believed L'Anse aux Meadows to be a whaling site. Then miraculously, a Nordic weaving spindle emerged from the earth. It was indeed an anomaly that a Nordic weaving spindle was found in one of the whaler mounds. Was it a deliberate twentieth century air transfer? There are thousands in Scandinavia. Locals think so.

Helge, being at the end of his exploration career, would certainly want a spectacular victory to justify his lifelong work, and northern Newfoundland needed an industry to compensate for a dying fishery. A marriage of convenience maybe?

The Micmac elders also told campfire tales of pale-faced men that landed at Milan Arm and collected berries. The Vinland chronicled in the Norse sagas did not refer to grapes but ripened gooseberries that grow all around the perimeter of Pistolet Bay that, when ripe, taste almost identical to wild grapes.

Bog ore could have been used by any of the Corte-Real expeditions or by any of the European settlers for making weapons, especially for whaling harpoons; the Strait of Belle Isle was a prime location for Basque whalers and fishermen. As for butternuts, even if not left by Joao Corte-Real, they float when dry, and the warm Gulf Stream could have carried millions all the way from New England to points deep inside the Arctic Circle. It is not uncommon to find flotsam in that area far removed from its source, even from Africa; it gets transferred to the Cold Labrador Current.

It took twenty years to convince the Canadian government of the Vinland site authenticity and even longer to convince the United Nations to make it a protected historical site.

But the open, honest people of Ha Ha Bay know the truth: history is what people write, the past is what happened; the dollar trumps the facts.

Chronicle 9

The Rock of Gold

All that glitters is not gold.

Top was accepted by his social group as a slow learner. His mother christened him Theophilus Barthelemew Higginbothm, but it took him eighteen years to learn to spell his first name, and that was only the short version, Theop, which he pronounced Te-op. As a result, everyone called him Top. He was a very loving and caring person who always tried to say and do the right things to please everybody. But people are cruel, and instead, he became the joke of the community.

Rumor has it that when Ms. Higginbothm was pregnant, she asked Mrs. Brewer, the preacher's wife, who was also pregnant at the time, when her baby was due in front of the church congregation, only to find out her baby girl was six months old. This caused Mrs. Brewer sleepless humiliation in a time when she had been boasting about her weight loss. This, in turn, infuriated her husband, and he brought the curse of the devil down on Mrs. Higginbothm, and Top was the result.

But Top did not give in to insults and jokes and soon caught the eye of the preacher's forgiving daughter, Ruth. She liked Top because he was kind, strong, and provided her with secret sex whenever she asked. In addition, he was a hard worker, very world wise, and soon built himself a fine house, and she asked Top to marry her. He readily agreed, and they were married by age eighteen.

Ironically, she liked Top to drink spruce beer and moonshine because when he was drunk, he was a remarkable, intelligent person. With his newfound respect for marrying the preacher's daughter, he soon found people buying him drinks to solve their problems, and he became known as gifted.

But his gifted mystique was soon about to vanish.

At the wake of Marley O'Grady, he drank a keg of homebrew just to see how intelligent he could become. Even though it was a brilliant moonlit night, on his way home, he fell into Marley's freshly dug grave at the cemetery near the seashore. As he climbed out of the pit, he had a vision from God. He saw a large rock of solid gold in the shallow water near the beach. He jumped out of the grave and ran toward his house waving his arms, screaming for Ruth to bring the wheelbarrow. After deciphering his excited bellowing, she informed him that she was nine months pregnant and was due at any moment. He told her to make the baby wait and get the wheelbarrow; the Lord had shown him where to find a solid gold rock.

His commotion aroused the whole community, and soon everybody was scurrying toward the seashore with wheelbarrows to carry their share of the sacred rock of gold. Ruth, who loved and trusted Top, realized he must have been drinking to be so intelligent, threw caution to the wind and grabbed a wheelbarrow, and wadded toward the beach where he was still screaming. She reached the shore with the others to see him pointing to a golden glistening rock on the reef. Everyone stopped and stared at it, spellbound. She jumped into the water and began to wade toward the moon-drenched rock.

With the excessive stress, her water broke and the baby began to come, and she called to Top for help. But he was adamant that the Lord wanted the baby to wait until he retrieved the golden rook. She had no reason to doubt him, so she continued toward the treasure. The mob followed closely behind in frenzy, all competing to claim the golden prize.

Panting and up to their necks in water, they all reached the site just behind a determined Ruth, only to find that it was a mirage above the calm waters caused by the moon rays reflecting off the rock and that Top was stoned drunk. As they embarrassingly melted away, they yelled and ridiculed Top.

Just then Ruth, with her head barely above water, stood still and smiled as she happily informed them that the baby was coming out. Stunned at her desperate situation, the women rushed to her assistance. Within seconds, she was holding a healthy eight-pound baby girl above her head and walking proudly toward the shore.

On shore, everyone again angrily turned on Top, heaping derogatory expletives at him, but he was paying no notice; he was ecstatically holding the baby girl, thinking it was the golden rock. Ruth, still with faith in him and belief in her god, rebuked them, explaining that the buoyancy and coldness of the water was God's way for her to give birth without pain, and God had used Top for his mission. The crowd scoffed, shook their heads, and filtered back to their beds. Ruth took the baby from Top and placed the newborn in the wheelbarrow on her wet clothes. She then turned to him, kissed him, and said sympathetically, "Don't mind them, they're ignorant fun makers. You'll always have me and Goldie."

Chronicle 10

Newfoundland's Biggest Wave

The Lord giveth and the Lord taketh away.

Tobias Taylor accidently met the love of his life in the most remote location and under the most embarrassing circumstances. He was seventeen and she was thirteen, with his father and the crew of his father's schooner, the *Cod Loader*, watching their escapade. It would be the start of an enchanting love story with a heart-wrenching end.

Toby was a shy, gentle giant who was homeschooled by a private tutor, a prodigious reader, and whereas most of his peers could not read or write, he was considered by them as a mommy's boy. His father found him surprisingly passive as well. He didn't drink or smoke and attended church with his three sisters and mother. Girls found him handsome, admired his muscular, rugged body, which was usually suntanned from not wearing a shirt, but considered him aloof and, being shunned, pretended to dislike him. He had never dated a girl, and when teased, he would confidently remind them that God would send him an angel one day, and until then he could wait.

Toby came from a well-to-do family in Ha Ha Bay, but his parents maintained a summer home at Port au Bras near Burin on the south coast where they fished after the northern fishery season ended. They owned a 160-foot Bank's schooner, which was captained by his father and, as of late, himself. Although studious, he preferred the rugged outdoor work of drying fish and stayed ashore whenever possible; seasickness was his curse.

After finishing high school, Toby's father, to make him more assertive, bequeathed him his most valuable asset, his schooner. As the only son, Toby respected his father's wishes. And by the fall of 1925, Toby had made his first transatlantic voyage as the captain of the *Cod Loader*, delivering his first cargo of salt cod to Spain. On his return, after being three weeks at sea without bathroom facilities, he was in dire need of a bath, and making landfall at Lord's Cove, where his father had friends, he hove to to give his crew a much deserved break.

It was a beautiful, warm autumn afternoon as he eagerly rowed ashore with his bag of clean clothes. Reaching the beach, a bath was the foremost on his mind as he excitedly stripped off his clothes and tossed it to the wind as he raced across the beach, sprinted up to the crest of the hill, across the buttercup field, down the steep ravine toward the pond swimming hole he knew, and dove in straight from the high embankment. After a long swim and a brief frolic, he thoroughly scrubbed himself and lay in the sun for a time to relax. Feeling clean and refreshed, he lazily began to stroll back to reclaim his clean clothes on the rowboat.

As he topped the steep hill unto the open meadow, he came face-to-face with the most stunning female he had ever seen. She was slowly meandering among the buttercups, lackadaisically following his trail of strewn clothes. The crest of her head was encircled by a halo of white orchids, buttercups dangled from behind her ears, and her long blonde hair fluttered gently in the breeze. In her arms was another large bouquet of multicolored flowers. She was dreamily pulling petals from a forget-me-not and singing sweetly, "He loves me . . . He loves me not . . .

The orange rays of the giant setting sun dispersed light around her body, silhouetting her against a crimson sky, making her appear to be floating on air. She looked like an angel, young, pure, and sweet. And she was completely nude!

She was jolted back to reality at his instant appearance, and in her embarrassment, all she could do was smile shyly.

He stopped, hypnotized, his mouth agape in astonishment, inhaling her stunning beauty. As she turned slightly, she appeared shimmering white, and the carved golden rays of the sun gave her wings. She was straight out of one of his Nordic storybooks, a Valkyrie sent by Odin to take him to back to Valhalla.

In his amazement, he forgot he was also naked. Recovering, and without a hint of shyness, he walked directly up to her and whispered softly, “Are you an angel? My pastor promised me one.”

Thinking he was joking and thankful for rescuing an awkward situation, she giggled and responded, amazing him further. “No. But my dad thinks I am. He named me Angela. He’s a preacher, and if he saw us like this, he’d set Satan on us.”

“This is my swimming hole, Angel,” he challenged teasingly to relax her.

“No, it’s mine. It’s on our property,” she joked truthfully. “Our place is just below the hill on the seashore.” She pointed in the direction but kept her eyes glued to his muscular body. Sensing he was aware of it, her face reddened; she giggled and added, “Do you realize we’re naked?”

“You’re perfect!” he responded emphatically, still enthralled by her perfect body. “Now I know why I waited.”

For the first time, he wasn’t shy around a female; he felt perfectly comfortable, as if he had known her all his life. He gently picked a sunflower stem from the bouquet of flowers covering her breasts, fashioned a crude ring, and kneeling in front of her proposed, “Will you marry me, Angel?”

She thought it cute, laughed, and replied jokingly, “Yes, of course, we’ve dated a long time. Ten or fifteen seconds? But I’m only thirteen, Dad would kill you.”

He got up and kissed her, his first kiss. She felt aroused and guilty at her carnal emotions but dropped her flowers, stood on her toes, put her arms around his neck, and responded willingly.

“How did you find me?” he then queried. “You followed my trail of clothes?”

“I followed the smell, and you were at the end.” She giggled again. “Who are you?”

“Toby Taylor from Port au Bras.” He pointed out the schooner below the hill. “That’s our family ship. I just came all the way from Europe without a bath. I’m the captain.”

“There’re no Taylors in Port au Bras!” she said dryly, insinuating he was lying about his captaincy as well but smiled at his attempt to impress her; boys often treated her that way, thinking a preacher's daughter was holier than other girls. She glanced at the ship and mockingly continued, "*Your* crew is looking at us through spyglasses."

He first felt uncomfortable that his father was watching him but proud the others were. He kissed her again to be sure they all could see him then casually directed her, "Let's get dressed and meet them. Where are your clothes?"

"This is our private property," she reiterated, "It's over in the buttercup field. I was going swimming."

She didn't know why, but for the next hour, she followed his every request like a little lost puppy as she toured the schooner. Seeing tough, rambunctious adult sailors, who were all noisy, drinking, and gambling, stop arguing and cursing and quickly stand up when Toby entered and then address him as *captain* really impressed her. He even had his own cabin, which was neater and tidier than her bedroom.

"They all listen to *you*!" she proclaimed later, astonished. "You don't smoke or drink? Are you an angel too? How old are you?"

"No, but I'm religious. Seventeen," he answered. "I won't boss you, Angel. You're my goddess."

"Angela," she corrected.

"Not to me," he retorted, kissing her again. "For the next eighty years, I'll call you Angel."

She blushed at the very ideas of being his wife but felt excited at the prospect. Thinking he was only kidding, she nearly fainted when he asked, "Can I meet your parents tonight?"

"You serious?" she almost screamed. "My parents will eat you alive!"

"They're cannibals?" he joked.

Even though the idea of meeting her parents thrilled her, she knew it was premature; they thought of her as an angel as well, and she needed time to condition them. Besides, her father was a pastor and had a virtuous reputation to uphold, and times were tough.

As they discussed it, Toby soon realized she was smart and practical as well as beautiful, and that made him want her more. He was determined not to let his golden opportunity slip away. Tomorrow he'd be gone, and he wanted to start a dialogue with her family; he knew religion as well as anybody and wanted her parents to know he was worthy of her.

Toby's father, overhearing the discussions, was sympathetic to his son's attachment to the young lady. He was relieved his son had finally found someone he liked and solved their problem for them. He sent Angela home to inform her parents of their casual encounter and that he and his son would visit the church later to pray and to make a generous donation to God. She was delighted his father so readily approved of them dating, but she knew with *her* parents, it would be a whole different story.

But the visit was successful beyond Toby's wildest dream. Angela's father and mother were in the church to meet them dressed in their Sunday finest. After attending a brief prayer and receiving the donation, the pastor insisted they stay for dinner.

Initially, the main topic of discussion at the dinner was the chance meeting of the children. However, Toby did not gain any merits from Angela for his unnecessary intimate detailing of their first encounter at the pond, but his honesty and religious reverence greatly impressed her father. She smiled devilishly, realizing Toby was more clever than him. And it soon became obvious to the Taylors that their affluence was a much more potent asset than Toby's piety, as the pastor constantly changed the subject back to their lucrative family business. By the end of the meal, Toby had gained the confidence of the preacher enough to date his daughter, unescorted.

It was the beginning of a magic courtship.

For the next six months, whenever the *Cod Loader* was in Port au Bras, Toby spent his free time alone with Angela in Lord's Cove. He afforded her great respect and was cautious not to make any undue passes to discourage her. He knew his donations to the church provided all the positive reinforcement necessary to sustain her father's blessing.

In the spring on Angela's fourteenth birthday, while on a business trip to St. Pierre, Toby took her and her family to St. Pierre for a week at his expense. There, Toby's dream really came true in grand style. One night at his hotel room, while their parents were at church, Angela came to his room and blurted out, "You're too good. Live. You do everything for me, I do nothing for you. I've been a virgin long enough. Make love to me, I'm like all other girls." Feeling embarrassed at her outburst, she whimpered, "That's all I have to give."

He was somewhat taken aback at her direct statement that he was too godly, even though she had inferred it many times. He knew he was too slow in seducing her; it was all part of God's plan for him. He hesitated, considered sex without marriage as a deadly sin, but could not imagine someone else having her.

Seeing his reluctance, she became embarrassed and, almost crying, asked softly, "I love you, Toby. Don't you want me?"

"I love you more than my life, Angel," he responded just as softly, caressing her tearful face. "Truth is, I've never made love to a girl."

She brightened up, kissed him, and giggled devilishly. "I'm no angel like you, I read a lot of bad books. I know how."

They lit a dozen candles, turned out the lights, took a small glass of the church wine, and lay on the fur rug in front of the burning fireplace. For the next hour in their romantic, idealistic paradise, he learned all he needed to know about lovemaking, uninhibited and unhurried. While he was naive and awkward in the art, she was not and directed him to the most enjoyable night of his life; she had indeed read a lot of books on the subject. It was the night of ecstasy he had always dreamed about. This was life at its best, heavenly bliss. Now there was no turning back for him; he had to have her for his wife. His life was progressing just as miraculous as God had promised him.

In August, when life seemed already perfect, much to Toby's disbelief, Angela asked to go to Spain with them for a visit, saying that her father had agreed on condition that his father was aboard as captain and would act as her chaperone. She wanted to cook to pay for her berth and, mockingly, help Toby with his seasickness. Toby knew his father considered them a perfect match and would agree, but it was reckless, almost heartless, that her father, a priest, would allow his only daughter to sail five thousand miles over rough waters to a foreign country at age fourteen with her boyfriend. Fall storms were sometimes deadly, and in the warm Spanish nights, pickpockets and criminals were everywhere.

Ironically, a week later, Toby learned from his mother that Angela's father was completely in agreement. It was Angela's mother who was scared of losing her. After exhaustive discussions on the details of Angela's safety while living among rum-soaked sailors and being given her own private accommodations, her mother acquiesced, and Toby was on cloud nine. However, Angela's parents didn't know she had concocted a plan all her own and that her berth would be Toby's cabin where she would sleep with him every night as his wife. After a year, she was now as madly in love with him as he was with her, and she wanted him all to herself.

Three weeks later in Spain, Toby took no part in unloading the salt cod; his father had ordered him to spend all his time touring the city with Angela. Never being away from home, the world was new and shiny to her, and she wanted to experience it all: museums, operas, movies, even bullfighting, which he detested. Shopping was her favorite, but she loved the enormous antique buildings, especially the churches.

One morning during their last week after business was completed, she insisted Toby wear the new clothes that she selected for him a few days earlier and that he accompany her to the church. Seeing her already dressed in her finest clothes looking ravishing, like the angel he first met, he could not refuse her anything. He was surprised to find the church almost full of worshippers so early in the morning. He coyly followed her straight to the altar where, to his surprise, the priest greeted her by name and asked her to kneel and pray. After which the priest smiled and directed her, "Go ahead, Angela, ask him."

She stood up and turned to Toby, blushing, "Toby, I'm sorry, I got pregnant, please marry me."

Toby nearly fainted. He was thrilled that she wanted to marry him, but being a father at his age was another issue. He wanted lots of children, but he was only eighteen and not sure he was responsible or mature enough. Whereas she was a gift from heaven, a dream, she was still only fourteen, and it wasn't his vision of marriage; he wanted a big family wedding with his mother and sisters present. He was left speechless. He wanted to say *yes* but not under these circumstances.

"Your dad already knows," she whimpered, beginning to cry, pointing to the whole crew in the front pews. "Mom will be thrilled. As for my dad, all he cares about is money."

"Yes, I'd love to," he began, holding her and wiping tears from her face as an enormous applause erupted from the congregation. "But I don't have a ring, I wasn't prepared."

"I have it," informed the priest, showing him the ring he made from flower stems, now dry and brown. Sensing disapproval in Toby's face, he added, "The good Lord sees only your love."

There was another tremendous applause and a standing ovation. Tears came to his eyes as well. He realized his father had known before they left home that Angela was pregnant and had colluded with her in making all the arrangements.

"Yes!" he announced emphatically, holding her hands and kissing her deeply.

"That's for later," informed the overjoyed priest, gently moving them apart. "Now stand together."

A hush fell over the building. A noisy photographer stumbled into position, dragging a load of gear. The organ sprang to life.

"Dearly beloved . . ."

From the ancient cathedral, Toby's father chauffeured them in a decorated wedding carriage with chiming wedding bells and drawn by four white horses on a roundabout course through the Lovers' Lane district of the city, with meandering tourists applauding and storekeepers tossing rice at them. Angela pondered how she had gotten so lucky; she was perfectly happy.

Returning to the hotel, they were ushered into a large lavish ballroom that was lit entirely by candlelight. In the center, there was a giant wedding cake with a dancing bride and groom on top. Rows and rows of tables filled with every kind of delicious food were positioned around the perimeter. Hundreds of guests stood at attention in columns that parted as they entered directing them toward the bandstand where a ten-piece swing band was playing their wedding march.

As they danced alone with the guests cheering, Toby silently contemplated why his life had become so perfect. More than perfect, it was excessive. God had indeed fulfilled his promise. But Angela was more practical and verbalized his thoughts. "How can your dad pay for all this? He must really love you."

He knew his father loved all members of his family, but how he paid for it he had no idea. Instead, he replied, "You're his family too now."

"I'll love you forever, Toby," she vowed, holding him closer. "But I don't know how long that will be, all those camera flashes are blinding me."

"And I promise I'll give all our children a wedding like this," he pledged, smiling. "All ten of them." Then as an afterthought, "You'll be my only love."

She held him close and replied, "Let's not live the future now. Tonight, all I want is your love." She paused. "And tomorrow a real ring."

Toby was surprised; it was the first thing she ever asked for.

Seeing his questioning face, she noted, "Not for me, just to satisfy my dad, he likes gold and status."

"My dad may be well-off, but I'm a pauper," he joked.

"We have the wedding suite later," she giggled, shocking him even more.

It was a wedding of legends, the type reserved only for the rich and famous, beyond their wildest dreams. Their life was indeed idyllic.

Three weeks later, as his schooner sailed into Lord's Cove, Toby was apprehensive, fearing reprisal from the pastor. But once again, God smiled on them. During the schooner's brief stop in St. John's, Toby's father had telegrammed ahead with the news. Arriving home, Toby and Angela were asked by Toby's father to first go to the church to thank God for their blessings. There they were astounded to see Toby's mother and his sisters waiting impatiently to hug them and a grand soiree prepared with all the community on hand to greet them. Angela's mother was ecstatic, her only requirement they be remarried by her husband.

The two-day celebration that followed was but another storybook fable for them. Toby felt his road in life was being paved with gold, and Angela felt everything she touched came up roses. They could do nothing wrong. And it was all because of their belief in God.

Toby and Angela settled temporarily into the Taylor winter home on the beach in Port au Bras until he had contractors build their dream home in St. John's to be nearer to his business base. It was a frigid winter, and Angela had a difficult pregnancy, requiring her mother to live with her, as Toby spent most of his time away fishing. Their perfect world was no longer a bed of roses, it was fusing with the thorns of reality, but their love for each other did not diminish. In fact, Toby had insisted the baby be born in a hospital in St. Johns, at which time his schooner lay in port for two days in prime fishing season as he paced the floor of the waiting room for his child to be born. And it was worth the wait. The child was a replica of her mother. Both were perfectly healthy.

The next two years flew by, and their life unfolded as God had promised him. It wasn't easy growing up and raising a family the same time with meddling parents, but love got them through the rough times unscathed, and by the last of September 1929, their new dream home had been completed in St. John's. The schooner was being loaded and moored just off the dock in Port au Bras with all their belongings, ready for the move. Toby's daughter, Patricia, had turned out to be the joy of his life, daddy's little girl who seldom left his side. Then more happy news; Angela was pregnant again. He anticipated a son.

November 18, 1929, found all of Toby's and Angela's relatives, plus a number of residents from the community, congregated at Port au Bras to celebrate their good-byes. Tomorrow they were all sailing to St. John's to assist with the move. A large bonfire burned outside the house on the beach. The children played some twenty metres away at the water's edge. Noise, laughter, and singing echoed across the calm bay. Shellfish boiled in large pots strung over the fire. The smell of jig's dinner cooking and partridgeberry pies baking filled the air. The weather was fair and calm with a full harvest moon overhead. Everybody was in an upbeat mood; everything was unfolding like clockwork.

At five o'clock, the ground shook violently, rattling the dishes for nearly half a minute, scaring the women. But most of the men, being outside and half-drunk—the preacher included—casually dismissed it as thunder from afar. Toby, in an unusual exuberant mood, to relax his pregnant wife, kissed her on the belly playfully, assuring the baby inside not to worry, that God would faithfully care for his followers, and that He was only acknowledging their farewell. Thus, the party continued unabated.

At about 7:00 p.m., Patricia went to her grandfather complaining there was no water to play in anymore. Following her back to the beach, he could see in the fading daylight his fully laden schooner on its side grounded on the bottom. It was the lowest tide he had ever seen; there was not a drop of water in the bay as far as the eye could see. He was first stunned then became concerned the rocky seabed could have punctured the loaded wooden vessel or the stress had broken the keel. It was an eerily strange sight, and it gave him a sinking feeling; it had all the earmarks of an impending hurricane. Looking up at the full moon, he relaxed a bit, guessing an extremely high neap tide would soon follow.

Sending Patricia back to the house with a friend, he took a group of his drunken sailors to inspect the vessel. Hearing all the commotion, the children soon assembled on the beach, making flares from the bonfire and running with them along the now fully exposed underwater sandbar. Others took the golden opportunity to collect more whelks, scallops, and mussels for the feast. Within twenty minutes, half the community was excitedly walking on the dry seabed enjoying the unique opportunity.

Again the earth shook, spilling the pot of boiling dinner over the campfire and causing some small rocks to come rattling down the hill behind the house, but it was very brief and less pronounced than the first. The women, terrified at the reoccurrence, now sure it was an earthquake, ran to collect the children off the beach. Angela quickly returned Patricia to her crib and warned her to stay there until she returned with her father.

As she walked on the seabed, she could feel the sand quivering under her feet and in the distance could hear the dull rhythmic pounding sound like a train engine approaching. The men figured the rattle had been a mild earthquake but of no real significance. Toby assured her that away from the steep cliffs on the sandbar was the safest place to be in an earthquake, so she hurried back to fetch Patricia from their house below the hill.

With no damage to the *Cod Loader,* the party resumed. Moonshine was passed around to toast their lucky stars, and the party settled in on the sandbar. Just then, ear-piercing screams erupted from a group of older children further out the bay. They were running near the steep shoreline and pointing to some object chasing behind them. Every eye strained to view the bizarre sight it in the dim moonlight. At the bay entrance was what appeared to be a huge white foaming wave moving at a terrific speed and gobbling up everything in its path. It loomed even higher than forty-foot Kelp Island and emitted a thunderous roar.

Toby's father, being the most experienced sailor, immediately grasped the situation. Pointing and yelling at the top of his lungs, he sternly ordered the children to get off the beach and climb up the hill, to which they scrambled without hesitation. He continued screaming instructions to the adults to help clear the beach, but nobody responded, failing to appreciate the scope of what was happening. It took precious seconds to forcefully compel the drunken revelers to move, and even so, most did reluctantly. He instead turned to the pastor and entrusted him with the responsibility of getting the few remaining younger children off the sandbar as he scrambled around the schooner in a panic searching desperately for his wife and three daughters who, with their helpers, were preparing the meal. He was mortified when he realized they were inside the schooner with the pastor's wife fetching dishes and utensils for the feast.

Toby was already racing full speed across the sandbar to catch Angela before she reached their house. His priority was to get Patricia and Angela to higher ground. Looking back, he saw the harvest moon illuminating the giant white-capped fifty-foot wave that was approaching like a speeding locomotive, creating a frightening resonance that vibrated the earth and echoed off the hills. It mingled eerily with the panic shouts of parents, desperate cries of children, and the howling of dogs. He could see the pastor had deserted his wife, was offering no help for the younger children, and was already running for higher ground.

The wave slammed into the schooner, crushing it like a matchstick, tossing it into the air, and summarily absorbing the pieces into the massive ball of debris that was being bulldozed ahead of the wave. The inebriated partiers simply disappeared into the mess without ever knowing what was happening.

Toby knew it was a tidal wave and was fully aware of its disastrous consequences. It was gaining too fast for him to reach Patricia and take her to higher ground, and he knew the house on the beach would be crushed or flooded.

Toby didn't feel the wall of water hit him, his mind was too occupied with Patricia, but he felt his face grinding into the sandy bottom, water filling his lungs, and then being tossed into the air amid other pieces of wreckage of his ship. Falling back down, his shoulder was smashed against a large chunk of debris, and a flying log snapped his left leg above the knee. Cringing in pain, coughing and gasping for air, he struggled to swim, but the pain was too great. Grasping a piece of flotsam, he held on and was swiftly carried along by the torrent, still searching desperately for Angela and Patricia, who were nowhere in sight.

In mere seconds, he was hurled past his partly submerged house, over the low-lying marsh behind, past the meadow, and up the gentle slope of the hill. Then, momentarily, the tide stopped. Frantically, he tried to swim to reach dry land just a few metres away, but his injuries were too severe, and the pause was too brief. The torrent began to recede. First slowly, then progressively faster until it reached the speed and violence with which it had entered. He became just another piece of driftwood in a massive pile of debris that was being siphoned back into the ocean, back past the harbor, the Head, Kelp Island. Finding a larger piece of white driftwood, he desperately tried to fight the undercurrent but to no avail. He saw boats, floating houses, animals, and people pass him in the mixture.

Everything was now becoming silent under the bright harvest moon. The water even felt warmer. He tried to climb upon a large chunk of his schooner to gain control, but his left arm had no feeling. He knew he was fading. He instinctively stared up at the bright moon in a blank stupor.

In his trancelike state, his three years of fairy-tale life flashed before him at the speed of light. He relived their first enchanting encounter, their courtship, their first awkward attempt at making love, their spontaneous marriage in a romantic old cathedral in Spain, his promise to his children, his nervousness of his wife's pregnancy, the joy of his daughter being born, his planned future in their large dream home full of children in St. John's.

He was jolted back to consciousness by the piercing, frantic screams of his pregnant wife near the shore and his terrified two-year-old daughter calling "Daddy" from somewhere over the water. The moving had stopped again. Unsure if he were hallucinating, he struggled to clear his mind. With the light from a gas lantern shimmering through a house window illuminating the calm water, he strained his eyes, peering into the darkness to gauge the exact locations. His pulse returned when he realized it was their home floating on the water nearby and Patricia was still inside. But to his horror, Angela was hundreds of metres away in an eddy being slammed against the rocks, and in his weakened state, he could only save one of them and began to panic. He took a few deep breaths, shook his head a few times to clear it, and managed to regain his sanity sufficiently enough to know he had to make a split-second decision.

Which one should he save? With a broken leg and injured shoulder, he was having trouble staying afloat himself. His daughter was younger; she deserved a shot at life. On the other hand, his wife was pregnant, two would die, and he could have more children, and she was still only eighteen. He soon realized debating life and death between two people he loved equally was morbid; it was playing God. What would God do? A more rational question, he rationalized, what lovable god would test him in such a manner? In his hour of need, God had deserted him just as God had deserted Jesus.

As he struggled to swim to the slowly sinking house, he heard his wife scream, "Someone, take care of Patty for me." Then as another giant wave hit, she gave a loud scream and disappeared into the pounding surf. That sound, and his fateful decision, would haunt him nightly for the rest of his life.

Smashing a window, he recklessly climbed through, inflicting a deep gash on his arm, but quickly located Patricia, who was still in the crib, her face barely above water and covered in blood. The stove had slid across the kitchen, crushing the crib, but everything else was intact. Thankfully, the house was floating nearly level with only a few feet of water on the floor, with the gas lantern still hanging from the ceiling. Lifting her from the crib, he soon discovered she had a piece of broken glass embedded in her face, a large splinter of wood protruded from her stomach, and she was losing consciousness. Dragging his broken leg, he scrambled with her up the stairs into their bedroom. He quickly removed her wet clothes and wrapped her in a warm wool blanket. Her arm was severely burned. He did not try to remove the foreign objects from her body since blood had congealed around the edges. Her heaving chest indicated she was breathing heavily, and gargling sounds were being emitted from her throat. It was a blessing she was now unconscious and felt no pain. He lay on the bed for a second to cuddle her and, within a minute, was unconscious himself.

Sometime later, he felt someone slapping him in the face and shining a light into his eyes. It was John Blake, their old fishing adversary from Burin, but it was the most welcome sight he had ever seen.

"I couldn't let you die, you bastard," John joked, smiling sarcastically. "I need competition. Now move your ass and get you daughter into the dory. Our schooner is standing by with a good midwife. That's all we bloody got. There's houses floating all over the bay."

Seeing Toby was incapacitated, they wasted no time, grabbed him, and threw him into the dory and placed the child on his chest.

As Toby and Patricia were being rowed toward the schooner, Toby noticed the moon had vanished; it had turned cold and was beginning to sleet. Dozens of dories with torchlights were rowing around and shouting, searching the black water for any signs of life.

"Wire St. John's for a good doctor," mumbled Toby, barely alive. "Patty's in critical shape. I can't find Angela—"

"Telegraph lines are down, there's a blizzard brewin'," John interjected mercilessly. "Pull yourself together, man, use the midwife or you'll both die. There's others in the same bloody boat."

Toby nodded robotically, his mind in limbo, as he talked to himself about his missing family.

On the schooner, the tired midwife worked almost mechanically as she removed the glass and wood from Patricia's body and sewed up the wounds with a needle and cotton thread and placed flour over the wound to stop the bleeding. It was far removed from her field of expertise, but she rationalized it might save Patricia's life.

With no painkillers, the midwife ordered Toby to drink whiskey before she started on his injuries; he flatly refused. With so many casualties to attend, she was in no mood for religious dogma. She had two fishermen hold him down as she forced about six ounces of whiskey down his throat then left to attend other victims. An hour later, she returned to a verbal, irate Toby spouting religion about how God would save his family, but she was overtired with no time, or sympathy, for his ideals. She had her helpers tie him down then stitched the gash on his arm, reset his dislocated shoulder, and splinted his broken leg.

For days, Toby hovered in and out of consciousness, and even when awake, he oscillated between a dreamworld and insanity. He ran a high fever, perspired profusely, talked continuously to his wife and daughter, prayed and sang praises to God.

Then one day, he awoke feeling almost normal in a hospital to see a doctor and nurse standing over his bed.

"Where am I?" he asked. "Where's my daughter?" Seeing their questioning faces, he added, "Patricia Taylor."

"You've been feverish for three days," explained the nurse.

"You're lucky," noted the doctor almost contemptuously. "Others are not. You're in an infirmary on a ship."

"What about Patricia?" he asked impatiently.

The doctor lowered his head and answered glumly, "We operated last night. I'm afraid she has serious internal injuries."

"What about Angela, my parents, sisters, the kids on the beach—"

"Get some rest," ordered the doctor.

That told Toby all he needed to know. He turned over and retreated into his dreamworld.

Toby spent the next two weeks in the hospital in St. John's recovering and praying by Patricia's side, but she was still in a coma when he returned to Port au Bras to attend funeral services, only to hear more unwanted morbid details. He stood shivering in the cemetery in the snowy field as his father, mother, and three sisters were buried together side by side in a single grave. But he felt no cold; tragedy had deadened his senses. He was unable to face reality, alone in his own personal hell.

"The Lord giveth and the Lord taketh away," Angela's father began, but Toby was no longer a believer. He was now totally alone with a single relative. Everybody else he loved was dead. His only contact to the past was the family photographs, which had been left behind in the house. His ship was lost without insurance, and anything valuable had been pilfered by the local residents. He was severely injured, and if his daughter survived, he would have to care for her as a cripple. No merciful god would permit such a horrific tragedy to befall his most faithful servants. And he could think of nothing more repulsive than Angela's father, a man of God, whom he so much respected, being a coward and deserting his family in time of need.

Due to communications outage, it required weeks to collect and interrupt the often contradictory piecemeal information to accurately determine the cause of the tragedy and for its full scope to became known, and it shocked the world.

At 5:02 p.m. on November 8, 1929, a 7.2 earthquake occurred at a depth of twenty kilometers along two faults beneath the edge of the Grand Banks, 250 kilometers south of Newfoundland. The earthquake caused a depression in the seabed, which in turn triggered a 250 cubic kilometres slab of earth to slide down the steep Laurentian undersea slope. The underwater landslide severed twelve transatlantic telegraph cables and generated a tsunami that caused local sea level to rise up to twenty-five feet. The first wave, travelling over sixty miles per hour, slammed into the closest point to its epicenter, the Burin peninsula of Newfoundland some two and a half hours later, increasing to a height of fifty feet at the head of several of the long narrow bays further inland; and Port au Bras was one of these communities. Two smaller waves followed the first. Several aftershocks, some as high as 6.0, caused several more tsunamis. The giant waves were felt as far away as Spain.

To add insult to injury, the next day it turned cold, with high winds causing sleet and snow to buffet twenty thousand homeless people, nearly half the population of the south coast. Twenty-eight people were dead and hundreds more injured. With no overland roads and the only telegraph line down, it was three days before the first word of the disaster reached St. John's, and an SOS was issued for ships in the area to render assistance.

The first help arrived late on November 22, an American ship, the SS *Meigle* with doctors, nurses, food and blankets. But with fifty outports distributed over a wide isolated area, numerous small communities would receive no help at all.

Toby Taylor's injuries healed within a few months. The body of his beloved Angela was never recovered. With international help, he quickly rebounded financially, bought a modern steel ship, and settled into his lavish dream home in St. John's with only her wedding pictures as memories and to care for Patricia. But Patricia spent the next four years in hospital and died in 1933 as a result of her injuries.

From that point, Toby's life changed drastically. Disenchanted with God and religion, he began to drink, smoke, and party heavily, daily reliving Angela's words, "You're too good, Toby, live." And live he did! "Live for today" became his motto.

Before he died recently at age ninety-two, he had dated hundreds of women but never remarried, saying he could never love anybody but his Angel.

And he became an antireligious crusader for the rest of his life.

Chronicle 11

How the Miracle Worker Lost Her Halo

Honor among the thieves: a convenient myth.

Aunt Jemima Blake was a saint. Acts of love fell from her hands like the warm, soft, angel-hair snow from an eager child's Christmas pageant she so often orchestrated. A devout Christian who could not say *crap* if her mouth were full of it. She was a ball of energy. To use her own words: 'The blessed Lord made me this way to serve others.' And serve she did. She helped everybody, not just the poor and needy. The church was the recipient of a great deal of her energy. In her first year as a member, she was given the prestigious position of organist, and if the church were happy with her, the people silently obeyed and revered her as a good person, and laurels flowed her way. And of course, money and service flowed to the church. The church was the law, next to the fish merchants. Any person who could extract the widow's mite from the impoverished fishermen of Ha Ha Bay was considered a gift from God by the church. Thus, she was referred to as the Miracle Worker.

And she was always contented and happy.

The source of her happiness was her beloved husband, Aldopohus, known affectionately as Alfie, whom she almost idolized. He too was a magic worker. A cut above the average, a model entrepreneur. She oft explained to the church congregation that it was God who had made him an honest, honorable man, blessed him with the gift of gab, and he used it wisely by convincing all the less godly men of the community to congregate at his fishing shed to study the Bible, give praises to the Lord, and raise money. He did it daily with conviction and enthusiasm. And she loved to sing along while working in the kitchen to the blissful sound from the worshippers echoing across the still waters from his fishing stage located a hundred yards from the house. They had a silent unwritten code of ethics. She would not interfere with his fishing techniques or friends, nor he her household methods or her friends. They stayed out of each other's domain. It worked like clockwork.

However, like most of the world in the late twenties and thirties, times were rough, and the source of Alfie's revenue to keep his wife happy was of a less pious nature. It was also a source of satisfaction for himself and his friends. The twenties also brought prohibition and rum running. Not being much of a sailor or fisherman and with liquor prices still too expensive in St. Pierre and Miquelon for a poor fisherman, he collected empty Barbados molasses containers, giant wooden kegs of three hundred litres, known as puncheons, and started his own in-house rum-running business on his fishing stage where he kept his nets and traps.

After the merchants had sold all the contents of the molasses puncheons, he would purchase them as vats for cod liver rendering and storage. And in all fairness, he did use some for that purpose, but only as a diversion.

When empty, the large empty puncheons typically had several inches of dense molasses dregs and sugar attached to its wooden walls. After estimating this amount, a task which he showed a natural talent, he would add the appropriate quantity of water and yeast for brewing, along with a few secret local herbs, then placed the keg among the covered cod liver kegs as concealment.

With his uncanny knack as a tinker, he built a first-class moonshine still and, using his gift of gab, in a short period of time, had amassed a few confidential friends to assist in his endeavor for just a few free swigs. News of the low-cost rum traveled fast, and soon he had a booming business in moonshine, even supplying the nearby communities. Brewed in oaken wooden kegs, it had a distinctive taste and odor, and it soon garnered a reputation of being the strongest and most palatable product in the area, creating a booming word-of-mouth demand. And at a reasonable price. To conceal his enterprise and to please his loving wife, he had his helpers sing gospel hymns as they worked, which became progressively louder as they became drunker.

Word of mouth of this sacrilege eventually reached the church, irritating the pretentious local priest. When the bishop responsible for the area dioceses called at Ha Ha Bay to collect the poor people's monthly tithes, the priest summoned Alfie and severely reprehended him for his evil, ungodly ways, a pretense to display his piety in the presence of the bishop in hopes of a speedier advancement to a larger church. However, he did not know the bishop was a classical shylock. The bishop charged for christening, for funerals; he enforced the 10 percent tithe and would charge worshippers a tax for merely existing if he could find a godly way to implement and justify it.

The bishop was reluctant to bite the hand that fed him. He had often wondered why the small parish of Ha Ha Bay was the most lucrative in the diocese. Somehow he had to maintain the status quo yet still be their respected, righteous leader. The bishop halfheartedly threatened to tell Alfie's wife and excommunicate both of them yet knew he could not carry through, since Alfie's wife was their prime fund-raiser and the church's only qualified bookkeeper. That would be suicide. He was at an impasse and angry at both his priest and the parishioner who had exposed Alfie.

With Alfie's gift of persuasion and cunning blackmailing tactics, he subtly convinced the bishop that his business was no more sinful than bingo or having sex with underage female parishioners, that selling alcohol was legal except that he paid no taxes, that moonshine, not fishing, was the source of his tithe that went to the church, and that he did not break any of God's laws since even Jesus drank wine regularly. He openly speculated that in return for the church's blessing, he could double his production and split the profits sixty-forty with the church.

The bishop quickly mentally calculated that since the church was presently receiving only 10 percent, should Alf quadruple his tithe, it would be a windfall. He was ecstatic. It was the opening he needed but was cautious not to agree implicitly in front of his virtuous priest. After a period of pensive silence, he smiled at his underling and mused aloud, "Brother, the blessed Lord's first miracle was to turn water into wine. Who are we, or the government, to question his mysterious ways? Render unto Caesar the things that are Caesar's."

The priest, grasping the bishop's aspirations, smiled at him approvingly.

Alfie reminded stoically, "Remember the good Lord's parable of the coins."

He had often heard his wife advocate sound business practices to him. However, he had no idea what the story was all about.

With an affirmative nod from all three, a business partnership was sealed.

For years, it worked like a charm. Most men in the community became involved in the secret enterprise. The Blakes soon became known as upper middle class and built themselves a larger home. Jemima was elevated to lay reader to keep her busy and away from home, thus preventing her discovering the secret. With the bishop's insistence, Alfie got her a servant to do her housework. The church prospered. The Blakes prospered. Soon they were shipping puncheons of moonshine to the rum-hungry Boston States.

Then in 1939, with a bang, WWII began. Alcohol became in greater demand, but Alfie, along with all of the other able-bodied men of the community, was ordered to volunteer or be conscripted. Most volunteered. This presented a major crisis; with all the men gone, the church would lose 90 percent of its revenue.

The bishop was adamant the church must not die and concocted a scheme to carry on Alfie's legacy. First, he applied to the military panel for an exemption for Alfie, implying that Alfie was a true conscientious objector who abhorred killing, a gentle soul who couldn't hurt a fly, who sang praises for hours each day to God. As a backup, the bishop got the dioceses' private doctor to provide a medical exemption slip to prove Alfie was unfit for combat, detailing how he often suffered from severe back problems, how he was often tired and spent several days each month alone in bed in the bunkhouses to prevent his lovely wife from contracting his mysterious affliction or from contaminating others. However, the bishop failed to mention Alfie's bad back was a slipped disc from lifting heavy puncheons, that his singing was to deceive his wife, or his debilitating disease was hangover.

Second, the church offered to supply good Jamaican rum to the troops on Cape Bauld at a 20 percent discount from their affiliated brothers in the West Indies. The military agreed and extended the deal to all its nearby installations.

Thus, Alfie was summarily exempted from the war, but these agreements presented a major conundrum for him. The deal had now made his enterprise a large operation. With the men away, how could he recruit and train females to do men's work? It was heavy work. He only knew a few women who drank. In addition, too many females helping at his storerooms all day would make his wife suspicious, or she would want to join their singing. He didn't want to break his well-functioning arrangement with his wife. Out of courtesy, he would be compelled to do housework, which he hated, or help with church functions, which he detested.

Then Alfie made his first mistake, a fundamental error. He broke the employers' cardinal rule: never employ a relative. Family success breeds contempt. Enemies can forgive you, but never your family. But with orders piling up and an impossible time schedule, out of desperation, he hired one of his renegade sisters to select and hire the appropriate women employees and his equally capricious cousin to transport the contraband.

Soon, with mushrooming business, he constructed a new larger summer fishing storage facility, conveniently concealed behind Burnt Cape, and moved his ever-mushrooming operation there. While it provided seclusion, transportation for his employees to the site became a major issue, and there was the matter of secrecy. How would he justify so many people just for drying fish? Especially on wet days.

Yet Alfie juggled them all; he was a superb organizer and a cunning manager. But an unexpected and potentially more serious problem soon appeared, one in which he had no experience: love and romance. It seemed whenever he extinguished one fire, another erupted. With women came romance among the employees; work became secondary. Besides, women gossiped and argued incessantly, whereas men just sang, boasted, or got drunk. Jemima had been his only girlfriend, and in matters of the heart, he left all decisions to her. Even worse, the romance was between his sister and his cousin. Both radicals and both inflexible. Alfie seldom slept anymore, most of his time was mediating disputes.

Within six months of the females arriving, he felt everyone knew of the operation except his wife, and he went through great lengths to keep it so. He now had thirty employees working around the clock. Whereas men mostly worked for free liquor, women wanted payment, which he had to pay daily in cash to prevent confusion and disagreements. He really needed an accountant to handle his books but knew it was dangerous for a bootlegger to keep records.

With all the people congregating at his large summer place, Jemima wanted to spend some time with them. She felt she was losing all her friends; they were becoming distant toward her, and the church was giving her more responsibility, even to affording her a helper, which she didn't want touching the books. Was it because of their newfound affluence? She sensed that something was amiss.

She had heard rumors that a lot of people, including women, were visiting his newly constructed fishing premises. She was positive Alfie would not cheat on her. She wanted to drop in to visit him, but they had an honorable agreement. Whenever her friends subtly inferred that something illegal might be occurring at the new site, as there were no fish, and her husband spent an excessive amount of time mending fishing nets, she chided them that a Christian wife must trust her husband, for better or for worse, and firmly reminded them that he provided nearly all of the funding for the church, who, in turn, helped the less fortunate. But, admitted she missed their gospel singing.

In August 1945, the war ended. Euphoria erupted worldwide. With money flowing, the bishop and the pastor took a month's vacation and left all the church functions in Jemima's capable hands, who had now been the lay reader for ten years. Life was good for her too, and she decided to have all her religious friends from the nearby communities organize a grand soiree to celebrate the event and scheduled it for Labor Day, which coincidentally fell on Alfie's birthday.

In a jubilant mood, Jemima invited everybody, all except the Newfoundland Rangers. She figured that she and Alfie had been separated long enough, and the time was ripe to change their agreement. Alfie needed to know the truth about her, that she was not perfect like he thought. With the war over, all the soldiers on Cape Bauld were given Labor Day off, so she invited them as well. It would be a grand surprise for Alfie, plus it would give her an opportunity to see the new fishing shed he had just finished without making him suspicious. She was mad with joy. Alfie was the perfect husband, a true saint.

But her saint was having insurmountable problems. His rebellious relatives wanted preferential treatment. This he could not fathom; they were already getting paid for doing nothing and siphoning off a portion of the moonshine on the side. And worse, his sister and his cousin had broken up and were in an all-out war. Even more ludicrous, the others wanted to legalize his operation and form a union. He felt he was losing control.

Upon Alfie's cousin's breakup with his sister, his cousin started pilfering an overgenerous portion of the shipments and selling it to anyone who would buy bootlegged moonshine at discount prices and keeping sales records under a fake company, which he called Jemima's Rum Distillery Pty, listing the church as the sales and distribution headquarters, hoping to piggyback on its success. The church was indeed coordinating sales, but only to the military from its fictitious company in Barbados through their equally fictitious mission and compensating Alfie, who in turn gave the prearranged percentage back to the church. Since the church didn't have to declare donations or pay taxes, the government revenuers did not audit them. It was designed to leave no paper trail.

Alfie was not a bookkeeper like his wife, but the disappearance of even one gallon of moonshine did not escape his keen business sense. He had a flawless system. Dried salted cod was sold by quintals, which was 112 pounds, and he had his homemade barrels or kegs constructed to hold 112 gallons, which he called a quintal, and used that term in dealing with liquor sales in case being overheard, it would appear as if he were conducting fish business. Thus, at ten pounds per gallon, a keg tipped the scales at 1,120 pounds, and he personally weighed every shipment for quality control. For every keg shipped, he threw a pebble into a paint can. He had kept a labeled dated can for every month since he started. He charged only for one thousand pounds to prevent any disagreement. Local consumption was strictly from the off-spec keg, which he called dregs. His limit of tolerance for skimming was 120 pounds per keg, which he called the devil's tithe. But his cousin had become too greedy and was misappropriating complete kegs, claiming they had washed overboard in rough weather, which Alfie knew was bogus since they were too large and heavy too simply fall off a boat.

Alfie recognized everything was spiraling out of control. His operation was now too large and no longer a secret. But he was an eternal optimist. Since the base was now closing, he would get a reprieve before his next venture. He speculated the pastor and the bishop's sudden disappearance together was not coincidental. The U.S. market was drying up too, but then again, soldiers would soon be returning from the war with modern ideas and likely heavy drinkers. All he had to do was hang on a few more months, control his unruly employees, and scale back his operation.

But most troubling of all was that the church left Jemima in control of its affairs. She was impeccably thorough; she would have to discover the companies in Jamaica were phony.

At daylight on Labor Day 1945, Alfie had just finished loading his large motorboat with ten kegs duly labeled Jamaican Rum, his final shipment for Cape Bauld, when several fishing boats appeared at his wharf loaded with people from the nearby communities, all of whom he knew personally. Before he could welcome, or question, the new arrivals, to his dismay, cutters from the Royal Navy, the Canadian Navy, and a corvette from the U.S. Navy appeared and anchored just offshore. It felt as if he were being invaded. All the young females went nearly hysterical with so many strong eligible military men available, dropped their work, and ran to the wharf to welcome them.

Alfie was furious. He guessed that his renegade cousin had set him up and, even though he was an eternal pacifist, for the first time in his life, grabbed another person by the collar and shook him. As the women were separating them, Alfie saw his wife with dozens of her church congregations appear from over the cape, all carrying food hampers and singing "Happy Birthday." His heart sank. He understood what his unsuspecting wife had done. Never did he have such mixed emotions. How could he explain all this to his beloved Jemima? The proof of his work was piled into his boat for all to see, complete with forged Jamaican shipping tags, which she would readily recognize. Inside, ten moonshine stills were in full operation. Dozens of puncheons full of brew were lined against the wall ready for distillation. He searched his brain for a logical explanation. All was now lost. He sat on a fishing buoy and covered his face with his hands to think. Spending time in jail did not bother him as much as losing his angelic wife; she had been the only girl who had ever paid him any respect. To him, she was as innocent as a baby and utterly naive about the workings of the real world. He would gladly protect her with his life.

Just when Alfie felt things could not get any worse, the ranger's patrol boat appeared at his wharf. He recognized that such a large congregation of authority was undoubtedly the result of a sting operation.

But Alfie was not one to admit defeat. The thought of losing his wife gave him renewed strength. He had only ten minutes to concoct a legitimate excuse. There was always a scapegoat; the key was to find it or him. He took a few swallows of strong moonshine, paced, scratched his head, looked all around, and viewed the desperate situation. Seeing his wife carrying a cross, he had an epiphany. It was as if a trumpet sounded heralding his innocence. The preachers had run away, and since the church was used as the transshipment facade for the rum, he could accuse the bishop and claim the church pressured him into operating their business under the threat of excommunicating his faithful wife.

He ran to his wife crying, knelt at her feet, kissed her hand, and began apologizing profusely. At first, she had no concept of what he was mumbling about. After a period of confusion and seeing all the equipment, she grasped the scale of what was happening. She then became annoyed he was drinking while working on his fishing equipment.

By now, a whole army of people, more correctly a navy, had gathered around as Alfie, who was kneeling, positively wretched, and grabbling in the dirt. Between his sobs, he explained to his wife and the rangers how the clergy was blackmailing him and forcing him to slave eighteen hours a day just to donate all his money to the church or they would expel her, how his relatives were also framing him and siphoning off any profits, how he was practically an overworked, broken-down pauper, and how much he loved and cherished her and would tolerate anything to keep her. The crowd stood listening spellbound as his charade went on endlessly. Some of Jemima's congregation and friends were crying at her husband's pathetic situation and his undying love for her. His flawless and unorthodox presentation touched even the rangers.

Nonetheless, the rangers halted the commotion and halfheartedly threatened to immediately close the distillery and confiscate all the assets as proceeds of crime. But the military personnel would have none of it. They didn't care; Alfie made the best rum. It was free. The war was over, and they wanted to party. And after a brief verbal confrontation, they carried the rangers on their shoulders to their patrol boat and told them to get lost. The rangers obeyed, not wanting to confront with drunken soldiers. The rangers too appreciated the war was over and wanted to party and wished so many people had not seen the operation, now they had to react.

And party they did. Within minutes, the kegs were broken open, fiddles and accordions sprung to life, and the large fishing shed became a dance floor. It became the biggest party of the century.

Alfie was astounded how cool and collected his wife could be under such adverse circumstances. Seeing him sitting dejectedly on his fake fishing nets, she called him aside and, amid the deafening noise of the drunken partying and carousing, tried to calm him by enlightening him on the more positive aspects of his predicament—none of which he saw—assuring him that the navy sailors would take away all the contraband in the cutters, including all the moonshine stills, and when they left, his problem would be instantly solved. He was completely at a loss to understand her ridiculous suggestions but was stunned when she nodded to the colonel, who directed some of his sailors to start loading all his valuable equipment into the boats without asking him. It broke his heart, but he could not disappoint his beloved wife.

By the time the rangers returned a week later, the place was a respectable fishing operation. Under an agreed code of silence, nobody would speak to the rangers except Alfie, who explained he was drunk the night of the party on church wine and he could not remember anything he said.

But with the clergy, there was no such honor among the thieves, and true to their credo, they tried to cover their tracks by hiding under the sanctity of the church. In the preliminary investigation, the clergy was difficult to locate but eventually responded through their legal counsel, stating that Jemima acted as bookkeeper for the church and as such must have acted as a front for illegal sales and money laundering of the money from her husband's illegal bootlegging operation and was apparently using the good name of the church. They even accused her of purchasing untraceable gold bullion through a high-ranking official in the military. They provided a written affidavit attesting they had no knowledge of such an ungodly illegal operation and had since moved to their new posting back in Ireland but recommended the new bishop taking over the diocese have the heretic Jemima expelled and charged.

Once again, Alfie figured he had accomplished the impossible, since due to his charade, the authorities considered him simple. As he kept no official receipts and was illiterate, he guessed the rangers had let him off the hook because they deduced it would be illogical to lay charges that would not bring a conviction, and he was deemed too incompetent to orchestrate such a sophisticated operation.

But his renegade sister and cousin were not so fortunate. The rangers found their records and, since both could read and write, were thus accused of forging church documents to facilitate an illegal operation. However, it was strange to Alfie that due to some technicality, they were never charged.

To Alfie, his most incredible discovery was that his wife forgave him without reservation, not even a complaint. For a month thereafter, he wanted to question her why she wasn't angry at him. She was smart, good-looking, a saint, and he had betrayed her trust. When he finally got up the courage to ask, she shocked him even more.

"Jemima, I love you, but I'm a fake—"

"I always knew you loved me, sweetheart. And I always knew what you did. You see, I hinted to the bishop two weeks ago that your cousin was framing him and that he had already informed the rangers on you. That way, I knew the bishop and the priest would disappear within a few days. I was the bookkeeper, the church did not know the value of your operation. You see, it was me who informed the rangers of your cousin's pilfering. That 50 percent was going missing."

"50? No, Jemima my love, only 10 percent," he cautioned meekly.

"I was the bookkeeper, Alfie dear, it was 50 percent."

Alfie, utterly confused, asked, "You scared the bishop away?" Then, recalling his wife's previous statement, exclaimed, flabbergasted, "You reported your own husband to the rangers? Oh, Jemima! You don't love me?"

"Yes," she answered calmly. "They got a small fee, but when your cousin informed them of your operation, then they were obligated to investigate. So I organized a big party as a charade and had the military show up—"

"The rangers . . . take . . . take . . . bribes? You talk to the military? What would they gain from—" he interjected, even more baffled.

"I was also the scheduler. I told the colonel you were shutting down the operation and he could have all the nonfixed assets for his assistance for free and—"

"What? That was twenty-one puncheons, nearly twenty-four thousand gallons of prime moonshine and ten stills!" he interrupted, gasping, now completely lost.

"Life isn't always what it seems, sweetheart."

"The colonel? That honorable person who's protecting our country is a crook?"

"Alfie, listen please. Try to understand. He was assigned to me by the church. He did all my banking offshore."

"Offshore? You mean he fishes offshore? He's a fisherman too?"

"No, Alfie. Thing is, you're now free. You went too far, you became greedy. God didn't like your excessive drinking. You were destroying yourself for me."

He knew that was correct. He stared blankly at her as if to say "You're truly an angel, I don't deserve someone like you." But he was still utterly baffled at her involvement in protecting him.

"Alfie, it's time for you to learn I'm no saint."

"To me you are, love." He reached out to kiss her.

"Alfie, please listen carefully—" she responded, pulling away for once.

"Jemima, sweetheart, please forgive me. I'm not learned like you but wanted to give you everything. Now we have a large house and property to keep up. I don't know how we will survive on just fishing, I'm not a fisherman. I worked hard but did not make much profit, the church took it, or that shyster that skimmed off the other 50 percent. He must have half a million by now."

"Almost a million. But not he, she."

"I was hoodwinked by a woman?" He felt crushed and embarrassed.

She finally smiled and noted gently, "You must know by now, Alfie, life's real, honor among the thieves is a convenient myth."

But Alfie's wasn't listening, his brain was working overtime calculating and recalculating his cans of pebbles and all the conniving, backstabbing, double-crossing rogues he had associated with over all these years. Who could be intelligent and rotten enough to rip him off for almost a million dollars over ten years? It seemed incredible. He tracked every shipment. It had to be some government fish merchant. Politicians and fish merchants were all damn shysters. He silently vowed before he died to find the bastard and smash her head.

"Do you have any idea who this millionaire is? Or what she did with the money?"

"Of course, Alfie. But the sanctity of the church prohibits identifying wrongdoers. We must forgive. God blessed me with fairness and integrity. Everyone trusted me without question. She has my trust. I wasn't just a lay reader, I was the bookkeeper, the scheduler, the clerk, the financier. That woman was—"

"Yes. Yes. I know all that, sweetheart," he retorted, exasperated and frustrated at being ripped off. If he could find her, he would give her a taste of his nonreligious version of forgiveness! "But what sleazy bastards took all our damn hard-earned money?"

"We did! It's in offshore, unmarked gold bars in our root cellar."

Chronicle 12

The Mighty Hunter's Trophy

Oh what a terrible web we weave,
when we first conspire to deceive.
—Walter Scott

Cain, who lived the life of hermit at the bottom of Pistolet Bay, was the prototypical free spirit and the quintessential hunter. He lived off the land. Literally. Yet a true nature lover who believed a person should take only as much from nature as needed for survival. And regardless of laws and regulation, he practiced it with reckless abandon. Avoiding store-bought salty, sugary grease balls—as he labeled most processed products—he believed big manufacturing companies had a secret agenda to slowly poison the working stiff and make him subservient, and viewed doctors as guinea pigs who naively dispensed medicinal drugs on behalf of the big drug conglomerates to unsuspecting people, solely for the purpose of addiction, thus ensuring their source of profits. The world consisted of a plethora of rich fat-cat conspirators in foreign countries to rob mankind of freedom. Yet he had never been more than fifty miles away from his birthplace.

He poached every locally known species of fish, birds, or animals for food as, and when, needed, but always taking only the amount needed and just the males to preserve the species. He refused unemployment or welfare, even old-age pension, saying a man who didn't work shouldn't eat. He has been found guilty numerous times for illegally catching shellfish, especially lobsters and whelks, which he loved, had been threatened with time in jail for killing seals, which he used for clothes a well as food, and was now on probation for allegedly shooting several moose. And once again he was claiming, as many times before, he had been framed by the system's lackeys. He owed thousands in fines but flatly refused to pay. The people, his pastor, or the courts could not convince him to respect conservation laws; he continued to live as man did thousands of years ago and exist directly from nature. He was born free and planned on dying free.

Lacking a formal education, Cain was not only at the mercy of the law courts, but also nearly every miscreant in the area who used him as a scapegoat for their misdeeds, as well as their source of entertainment and jokes, but always behind his back. His being big, cunning, and tough as nails prevented anyone from confronting him directly; instead they secretly contacted the local authorities to report his infractions.

Shunned by most of humanity, he lived alone in his large log cabin with his two Newfoundland dogs, yet in spite of his degradation, he was open and honest with people he could not avoid and treated them with respect but trusted nobody. But most of all, he was an incurable collector. His large fishing shed, his garage, and his home were all clustered with antiques, ranging from trinkets of local shipwrecks, such as a compass from the SS *Langleecrag*, movie posters of old western movies, to animal antlers, which adorned the walls of each of his buildings.

Cain was religious and lived by Bible teachings, which was the source of his tenacious resistance. The only person who proclaimed to understand him was his Pentecostal minister, who accepted his negative assessment of mankind and who also professed to believe in his protestant work ethic. The preacher, Rev. Kinchella, was not as loving and forgiving as Cain and convinced him to make use of his unique outdoor skills and wisdom to set a trap and catch the real moose poachers. Cain was over seventy, but he had the stamina and looks of a forty-year-old, thanks to his healthy outdoor lifestyle, and with his uncanny knowledge of wildlife, he knew he was easily capable of baiting such a trap; he followed everybody's misdeeds.

Cain's nemesis was the local game warden Phil Coombs and Phil's relative Edgar Pelly. They were inseparable; even their wives were best friends. And this year, Phil felt extremely lucky; his customary summer helper was a naive forest and wildlife warden trainee from Memorial University in St. John's, an egotist named Clyde Stevenson.

Clyde's mandate was to shoot moose with a tranquilizer gun, tag them with GPS monitors, and record their habits for the Wildlife Department; and as an experiment, he was to stream his findings to the university facility live via the Internet for his MBA zoology thesis.

Phil reasoned Crazy Cain, as he called him, would poach one of these moose and hang the antlers on his wall, and the GPS locator would act as positive proof to convince the capricious courts. In the past, each time Cain had appeared on a charge, he would accuse him and Edgar of framing him, that they were the real poachers, and the judge was becoming increasingly suspicious. This way, they would get the nuisance out of their hair once and for all.

For the next week, Phil and Edgar did nothing but drink as they honed their flawless strategy to ensnare Cain using the green college warden. But Cain, with the preacher's insistence, managed to organize a secret meeting with Clyde first, warning him that Phil and his friend were the real poachers and that they would likely frame him as well.

Clyde, being a high-strung overachiever from a rich arrogant family, was incensed at merely the idea of being a scapegoat. Clyde distrusted the preacher; he had a condescending air about him but liked his flirty young daughter who regularly came alone to his wildlife cabin to borrow his rugged outdoor clothes, often changing in his presence to entice him. He wanted her just as badly, but she was too young, and several times, he almost faltered. Nonetheless, he gave her everything else she asked for.

Being well indoctrinated by Phil on Cain's history of illegal activity, Clyde was indecisive. He saw Cain as an independent, uneducated simpleton who followed no rules of civil society, but in the end, grasped the opportunity and decided to teach them all a lesson, and with Cain's practical understanding of animal movements in the area and his own technical knowledge, he concocted an ingenious plan to test Cain's conspiracy theory to catch the poachers red-handed while at the same time taking his thesis experiment to the next level.

In the next two weeks, with Cain's assistance, he tagged five moose with white tags, which he labeled Phil's Moose, and on a separate outing with Phil, he tagged an additional five moose with yellow tags that he labeled Cain's Moose. Unknown to either Phil or Cain, he equipped all ten moose with miniature video cameras to record their mating habits, rationalizing that it would be accepted by the university as extra credits for his degree. To gain even higher marks, he streamed each camera to a separate YouTube site then advertised all these sites in both the local media and the student council newspaper. He wanted instant recognition for his brilliance, and this would be the most glorious way to show his contemporaries how he caught the poachers in the act.

When September came and the hunting season started, Clyde informed Phil, Edgar, and Cain that he was closing the wildlife cabin for a month to return to university. Nobody had cause to disbelieve him; after all, he was a student. He then retreated to his cabin to secretly monitor his operation.

As was Cain's yearly ritual, each year he killed a small male moose, cautious not to select the white-tagged moose, bottled the amount he needed for the winter, and gave the remaining portion to the preacher to be distributed to the less fortunate. Clyde did not intervene; Cain had warned him he would poach a small male. But to his astonishment, Cain did not mount the antlers on the wall of his fishing shed with his other collectables; instead he gave it to the preacher.

After a month alone in a small cabin without the preacher's chatty daughter visiting, Clyde developed cabin fever. The results of his experiment weren't materializing as rapidly as he had anticipated. Each moose had a mind of its own, and they followed no discernable pattern. Realizing monitoring was going to be a slow process and that he was becoming too obsessed with the early completion of his master's degree, he decided to take a two-week holiday to Hawaii to relax and record the results of his experiment in his absence. Since he lived in a wildlife cabin instead of the projected motel, he could use the excess living allowance portion of his university-sponsored grant to pay for the trip; the university would never know.

In the warm sunshine, Clyde enjoyed all the amenities Hawaii had to offer and put his experiment completely out of his mind, refusing to even take a computer along or watch YouTube. But on his return, being rejuvenated, he was anxious to get back to work and view the results of his recordings. To his utter surprise, he was met at the airport by his irate degree sponsor from the university demanding an immediate explanation for his actions. By his side was a stern-looking police officer.

"Who authorized you to post university findings on the Web?" the sponsor demanded without any greeting.

Only then did Clyde remember that the videos were still being streamed live to the Internet. He was surprised and somewhat irritated, especially in light of all the extra work he had done. What could a moose do illegally?

"We have some questions for you regarding Rev. Kinchella and his daughter. When you get settled, give the office a call. Don't leave town without consulting us," ordered the police officer, giving him his card and departing.

"Phil knows more about Rev—"

"Mr. Coombs and Mr. Pelly are in custody," the officer retorted.

"What's the problem?" Clyde inquired, dumbfounded. "A moose get one of Cain's dogs pregnant or—"

"No! But the preacher's underage daughter might be," snarled the sponsor. "You watch the tapes. All of them! Then talk to our lawyer. First thing you're going to do is shut down those damn YouTube websites."

"I was in Hawaii—"

"Yes. Unauthorized. That's an order," injected the sponsor. "And say nothing to anyone—"

"I don't know anything to say," interrupted Clyde, now angry.

"If you don't want your program cancelled, shut up," retorted the sponsor, walking away. Looking back, he ordered, "And watch those tapes tonight. The university lawyers will want to talk to you tomorrow."

Clyde was tired upon arriving at his cabin but shut down the eight websites, which he noted were already displaying blank screens. In his absence, someone had perched a moose head with antlers over his mantelpiece. That was somewhat troubling since he had placed the cabin off-limits but guessed it was Phil, since he had unlimited access to the government wildlife cabin most of the year, but he was too tired and angry to watch the tapes, so he had a drink of rum and went to bed.

Next day, Clyde sat with the university lawyer watching spellbound the results of the ten tapes. To his dismay, all ten of his experimental moose were killed while he was on his illegal holiday, most killed by people in whom he had confided the whereabouts of the moose and who were held in high esteem by their communities. He did not have a single moose mating ritual to show for his thesis. But he did have human mating rituals. It appeared that hunting cabins were not only favorite places to mount antlers, but also favorite places to make moonshine, party, and have sex. And most shocking, group sex. At least twenty people were involved, all of whom he knew, and it was assumed the authorities figured he had orchestrated the trysts in order to surreptitiously record and stream underage pornographic pictures to the Internet. He could easily understand their reasoning for wanting to question him. The quality of the recordings was crystal clear and, to his horror, sexually explicit. The camera was strategically mounted as if done by a professional photographer.

On one tape, he saw Phil and Edgar kill two tagged moose with white tags. On another, he saw Phil having explicit sex with Edgar's wife in Edgar's own cabin. On another, to his horror and most disturbing, was the preacher's daughter, a girl in whom everybody knew he showed a great deal of interest, having sex with Edgar, who was twenty years older than her and married. He shuddered when he realized it was in his cabin and she was wearing some of his personal clothes. He was now positive of the real reason he would be questioned but had no idea who mounted the antlers there.

Just as shocking were videos of the pastor selling marijuana, ecstasy, and other illegal drugs to minors. The language, threats, and innuendoes used by the pastor were almost bloodcurdling, subtly warning anyone who talked would go missing some foggy night in the marshes.

However, Clyde found two of the tapes somewhat entertaining. In one, a person gave the antlers to his friend from British Columbia, and the GPS monitor tracked the moose, making it appear to swim across the Cabot Straight and run all the way across Canada. The lawyer explained it became a news media sensation and had a large following that amused everyone watching, except his prestigious university facility, which bristled at seeing its insignia and motto being so prominently displayed on trivial videos.

In another, a group of tourists stood in the highway taking pictures of two moose as one turned toward the camera and gave an oversized dump.

After a full day of watching the videos, Clyde was inundated and wanted no to see no more. He wanted answers and blurted out, "Enough! Tell me what happened to Cain. And the pastor."

"The pastor is being charged on eighteen accounts of drug trafficking. Among others."

"I never trusted him. But good Lord, eighteen?" There was a period of deafening silence as he dejectedly stroked his hands through his hair. "And Cain?"

"He's shot a moose, all right, you knew that. He cooked a delicious sirloin steak from it for me," answered the lawyer, sounding conciliatory. "Still, he's an honest and trustworthy man. The very salt of the earth."

That Clyde had already learned, but his overinflated ego would never let him admit it. He waited for the punch line.

"He's willing to testify against everybody, including you," continued the lawyer casually.

"What can he tell about me? We just tagged moose together."

"He didn't trust you, the pastor even less. And like all the others, you grossly underestimated his intelligence as well. He knew you colluded with Phil in tagging more moose, that you put cameras on them. That's why he gave the antlers to the pastor, usually it was only the meat. Cain likes his trophies. You knew he was a collector. All the local people knew the pastor was selling drugs. Cain just framed him by mounting the antlers in a prominent position in the pastor's shed for best public viewing; by the world in this case."

"You mean he helped the hunters to find the moose? Even Phil and Edgar?"

"Pointed out the exact ones you tagged 'Phil's moose'. White tags are easy to spot. Police has them."

"Cain is a habitual scavenger. What the hell was his motive? Revenge?"

"Not in his nature. Truth. Doesn't even want his criminal record to be expunged. Just the right to catch fish and wildlife for his own consumption until he dies."

"No court will ever agree to that. Cain's not that smart."

"No? You, above all, must know most learning doesn't come from books. You're confusing wisdom with knowledge. He knows this bay like the palm of his hand. He trapped all his enemies and you. Including the respected preacher. The courts have already tentatively agreed in return for his testimony. Not such a stretch, he's seventy-two."

"Why charge me?"

"You want the synopsis or the ten-page detailed list?"

Clyde guessed most of the offenses and remained quiet.

"Let's see?" he continued. "Possible underage sex or interference? Illegal use of university funds? Entrapment? Posting porn on the Internet, possible fraud—"

"Who put that goddamn camera in my cabin? The police?" He asked angrily, concerned he would now be charged with statutory rape.

"Cain. Who else? He told the police he did what you told him: to give you all tagged moose antlers he found for your thesis. Someone else killed them. You all betrayed him, but he trapped all of you in your own web of deception." Then musingly added, "Cain was truly a mighty hunter."

Clyde was flabbergasted but sneered, "Really? What was his mighty fucking trophy?"

"Simple justice and freedom. Rare commodities these days." Seeing Clyde defeated, he inferred insultingly, "Aren't they?"

Clyde was too crushed to speak. He put his hands on his bowed head and took an exhaustive sigh.

"My mandate was to show you the tapes. They are university property and will stay in my custody until trial. Watch them as often as you can. Closely. Remember police have an office copy for your viewing. This is all the university will do for you. From now, you're on your own. Close down this cabin within a week. Do yourself a favor. Get your rich daddy to supply you a good lawyer. The university is not in your court. It's going to be a bloody mean free-for-all."

Clyde appreciated the frank prognosis but said nothing as the university lawyer left. He knew the next three months would be a nightmare for him. The public loved scandals, and while he awaited trial, the rumors would likely skyrocket out of control, and his reputation would be in tatters. He pondered how a modern, logical, analytical scholar like himself could have underestimated an old uneducated bozo so badly.

A year later, the trial became the biggest event of the decade in the area. Seventeen people were charged, each with a litany of offences, and the circuit courtroom was filled to overflowing, everyone anxious to hear the sleazy details. Disappointingly, most plea-bargained and admitted guilt in favor of lighter sentences, probation, or to escape a criminal record and, as such, prevented the humiliating details of their actions from reaching the public.

All except for the preacher, Phil, and Edgar, that is. Phil and Edgar's imbroglios became the subjects of hero worship by the men, whereas the preacher was reviled by all as a lowlife. Awaiting trial, Phil and Edgar became bitter enemies, spilling every lascivious detail in a tit-for-tat one-upmanship and eventually testified against each other in court. They each received six months in jail for breach of trust, poaching, and a host of lesser wildlife violations. Phil got an additional two years for statutory rape. Both would be divorced shortly thereafter.

In light of his respected position in the community and his influence over youth, Rev. Kinchella was sent a strong message and sentenced to two and a half years in federal penitentiary for selling illegal drugs and was thereafter stripped of his clerical position and ostracized by the church.

Clyde was not charged but became the butt of barroom jokes for refusing to have sex with the preacher's beautiful young daughter. At a preliminary hearing, Cain vouched for Clyde's innocence, and in an unusual verbalization in his own vernacular, testified that "Clyde was just a snotty college know-it-all smart-ass rich brat who had no responsible parents to give him a swift kick in the arse and, because of that, had none of God's good sense or doable life experience in a rotten world and, deserved a second chance." The judge agreed and placed Clyde on probation. However humiliating, Clyde was eternally grateful to Cain for that derogatory statement, but his university, who had a reputation to uphold, was not as forgiving and expelled him, demanding full repayment of his research grant.

In appreciation, the court offered to expunge Cain's previous convictions, but he refused. His victory had absolutely no effect on him; he continued to live and poach as he always did. He became the undisputed folk hero, but he took it all in stride. However, he did appreciate the way people now treated him.

But he was never again accused of any wrongdoing.

Chronicle 13

Saint Brendan Discovered Newfoundland

Truth is stranger than fiction.

Shamus O'Toole was Irish. So fanatical was he that his dear ole Erin zeal made St. Patty look like a Muslim heretic. He loved his Irish whiskey, was never seen without green trousers, wore a cap with a green shamrock and a shirt with an embroidered green leprechaun. His favorite meal was mutton and onions with lots of potatoes. His music was always accompanied by the accordion, the flute, or the fiddle. His fishing boat was painted green with the name *St. Brendan's Isle* prominently displayed on the stern and both sides of the prow, which he claimed was Newfoundland.

Shamus, known as Patty, as was every other Catholic in Ha Ha Bay, spent his idle time drinking his home-brewed vodka, which he distilled from potatoes and which he claimed was good Irish whiskey. His easygoing magnetic personality and his free moonshine attracted lots of friends.

But first and foremost, Patty was a storyteller. When drunk, which was often, he recounted epic sagas of Ireland with such dedication and sincerity that even the most outrageous anecdotes would seem plausible. He was fairly well educated for his day and had travelled widely in Europe before coming to Newfoundland to fish, where few could read or write. Even though he was now over seventy-five, his command of history and his ability to narrate the unrecorded legends of his ancestors were both impressive and inspiring. He would alternate between knee-slapping laughter and mournful funeral wails within seconds while reliving his country's tragic history. And in the winter off-season in Ha Ha Bay when there was no fishing, he was the community entertainment and had ample time to relate his favorite epic tale, a two-hour marathon on how St. Brendan discovered Newfoundland. So compelling was this special chronicle that it fascinated the whole community even after decades of telling. No one spoke or went to the bathroom for fear of missing a syllable. The drunker Patty became, the more emotional and spirited would be his presentation. At times, his gestures, voice inflections, and dramatizations added more credibility to his tales than his words.

"Me great-grandfather was born in Tralee, County Kerry," Patty always began as a prelude to his legend. "Like me grandfather, me father, and meself. You see, we're all direct descendants of St. Brendan. No farmers, us."

He would then pause, settle comfortably on his three-legged stool at the head of his large share fisherman's bare wooden meal table in the middle of the open bunkhouse and slide a naggin of moonshine to anyone present. Anyone left standing would scurry to the table to be near him; then the room would go deathly quiet.

"The blessed Virgin sent a bright light to illuminate the mud barn to announce Brendan's arrival, just like that Star of David for Jesus," he then continued, crossing himself, standing up briefly, and removing his tam-o'-shanter out of respect for the dead. "The year was 488. A year foretold by St. Patrick a hundred years earlier.

"Was baptized by the great bishop Erc himself. The heavens had revealed the signs to Erc in a dream that Brendan was a cut above mere humans, some sort of god. So after only one year, he took the child from his parents and sent him to Saint Ita in Killeedy, who for five years took advantage of Brendan's gifted powers to protect the town against those bloodthirsty Viking invaders who pillaged the coast every year, as well as the to ensure a good harvest, but still found time to teach him the ways of the gods, which some say he was.

"At only six, Brendan was returned to Erc to be ordained as a priest and to be an understudy to the saints. Brendan's fame spread fast. Attending *that* ceremony was all the great Irish saints of the time. They all travelled great distances, proud to be there. Finnian of Clonard, Enda of Aran, Jarlath of Tuam, among them."

He paused, took a deep breath then a swig of moonshine, and shook his head.

"Why did Saint Ita return him you ask?"

Nobody did. Patty often filled in his audiences' questions as a means of sensationalizing and dramatizing his story.

"You see, Brendan too had a dream at age three: to travel to the four corners of the world and set up monasteries to help the poor and spread the story of the Blessed Virgin Mary. He was told he would sail far over unknown seas and find the Promised Land. And Saint Ita was fully aware nobody knew building curraghs and travelling afar more than Erc. Had sailed all around Europe, knew the lay of the land by heart.

"You see, back then, they didn't have motorboats. All they had was curraghs, small—say thirty foot—open boats with wood frames, covered with ox skins, and sealed with pitch from the bogs. With only an ox-skin sail and a few oars for power. Compasses weren't invented, they sailed by the stars or were led by the angels.

"But first, little Brendan had to be educated. For that, Erc was the master too. Smarter than all those saints who often sent students to him to be taught on how to survive the heathen ways of the cruel world. And they say by the time Brendan was ten, he could read all the then available monasteries' scrolls that were written in the ogham script, the only alphabet they had at the time. The heretic Vikings having had destroyed most of them in their raids to light their cooking fires.

"Erc, though a bishop, was more practical than religious. 'God helps those who help themselves' was his philosophy, and he imposed it on his disciples unmercifully. A giant, tough as nails. And young Brendon, by the age of eleven, was no slouch either. Showed the lad how to build curraghs. Made him do all the hard work too. Caught on fast like a veteran. Within a year, he knew how to sail them by the heavens at night. Knew all the major stars from memory. Could tell you where they should be every day of the year. But the North Star was his talisman, it never moved. Fools can sail by day, Erc convinced him, sailing at night takes skill because there were always leprechauns and banshees to be held at bay. Bastards for playing tricks on your mind. Fairies were bad too. Erc sent him alone on journeys for weeks.

"By this time, all the people began to realize Brendon was saint material and began to follow him as his disciples. With his smarts, Brendan soon took advantage of these monks, chose the strongest and smartest to build even larger curraghs with two sails, and with Erc's directions, set off on a journey to Europe.

"For twenty years, Brendan roamed the coast of Europe, carefully avoiding areas of war and strife. He was a peaceful man, his mandate was to set up monasteries to educate local monks about the true God and teach them how to help the peasants. He travelled to England, Scotland, the outer islands of the Hebrides, even to the Faeroe Islands. Travelled to Rome, met the pope, who offered him a position in the Vatican, but Brendan gracefully refused, explaining God had preordained him a mission to travel and explore all the lands of world until he found the Promised Land of the saints. This greatly pleased the pope, who gave Brendan some generous funding and his blessing, even promising to send his most learned scholar to write his memos upon completion of his pious mission.

"Brendon had a gift for understanding others. A good listener, seldom talked. Soaked up all the knowledge he could from all the old seafarers he met, questioned them on their expeditions, and made many improvements to his ship. Learned the earth was round. Heard heart-pounding tales of luscious lands filled with milk and honey, about rivers full of gold and riches far to the west from the Phoenicians, and romantic accounts of an industrious, advanced civilization of small yellow peoples who lived in golden palaces from the black Arabs, who claimed they had travelled all the way to the western ends of the earth on their camels by travelling overland to the east.

"Such fables encouraged Brendan, but he believed charity starts at home. He first returned to Ireland around the year 540 and organized numerous monasteries throughout Ireland. Founded a convent in Annaghdown, County Galway, where his sister, Big Brig, was the curator. Just as tough as he was. But the grandest was in Clonfert, not far from Annaghdown. Used magnificent designs from the great buildings he saw in Italy. Been in that building myself, a marvel of architecture. Became one of Europe' s most influential schools until Henry VIII wanted to divorce his brother's whore and fucked up the Catholic Church in England then forced their Protestant heathen ways on the Celts in dear ole Erin."

Patty took a drink of moonshine and paused to gauge the reaction from the Protestants in an audience that was now standing room only. But nobody else in the room was religious except Patty; they were only interested in listening to his yarns or drinking his moonshine.

"But Brendan was, most of all, a wanderer, seafaring was in his blood," Patty pressed on. "By now, he had thousands of followers. Taught them to build the largest curraghs ever dreamed of in Ireland. On Good Friday, he took seventeen of the most seasoned monks and sailed directly west. But they met storm after storm, the devil fought him every step of the way, and after forty days and nights, they began to run out of food and water, were forced to return to Ireland to plan a different route.

"As Brendan weighed his options, he recalled while in the Faeroe Islands on a previous voyage hearing tales from the people about a land to the northwest that could be seen in the sky on hot summer days. He figured that must have been God's vision of the Promised Land that was to descend from heaven. He set out again with the same experienced crew and, using island-hopping, sailed to England, Scotland, the Hebrides, Orkneys, Shetlands, and back up to the Faeroe Islands, which he reached by mid-June.

"There Brendan conversed in private with a most unusual monk. The bishop, who was assigned to run Brendan's mission from his previous visit, warned Brendan that this unique, boastful monk was touched by the fairies or was a servant of the devil. This monk, who was not a farmer but a fisherman like Jesus, related an epic journey of how he had been to an island not far to the north where there were lots of fish. Had gone ashore there and met strange sealskin-clad heathens who ate raw meat but were yet very sociable and friendly. The heathens wanted him to take them home to where their ancestors lived, an expansive island even farther away to the northwest. Said it was dark all winter, yet in summer at midnight, it was bright enough to the kill lice on one's clothes.

"Brendon stayed for a fortnight and questioned the fisherman monk often, in great detail, and found him intelligent and knowledgeable but, at times, having delusions of grandeur. The strange monk cautioned Brendan that the island where the heathens lived was near hell, and it sprouted fire from the top of huge mountains night and day, preventing anyone from landing near its shores. Brendan was cautious. He doubted if there could be more islands even farther to the northwest, the earth was only so large.

"But the crazy monk was adamant, explaining that all Brendan had to do to find this land to the north was to follow the flights of the migrating birds, especially starlings and other small land birds that could not land on water; or follow the cloud formations, which moved mostly from the south in spring and from the north in the fall. That in itself was proof they were going to the island. Said if you followed the birds during their spring and fall migration, the winds would take you there and back. Same every year, regular as clockwork.

"Brendan was convinced. He figured if he could get to this hell, the Promised Land could not be very far away, maybe the land to the northwest. He hastily reprovisioned his ship, took the crazy monk as his guide, and immediately set sail for hell.

"Late one moonlit night during a gentle breeze when all hands were asleep, after just one week at sea with favorable wind, they were all jolted awake by a thunderous roar. They quickly arose to see a huge yellow glow illuminating the seas and a mountain peak towering above them sprouting fire into the heavens, warning them to stay away. Brendan was jubilant, he knew he had reached hell. Confidently, he took out his cross, pointed it at the fire, and called on the name of St. Patrick to force the devil to stop. But much to his chagrin, it didn't work, the mountain became angrier. However hard they tried, they were unable to go ashore, the sea around them was a cauldron of churning, boiling water with blinding steam, and they were being bombarded by large chunks of fire from hell. Flung down at them from the top of a high mountain. The smell of burning brimstone nearly poisoned them. Went dizzy headed. Brendan even saw Judas Iscariot clinging to a rock, trying to escape hell.

"Brendan was not one to admit defeat. He sailed a hundred miles along the coast and found a beautiful sheltered steep-walled fjord with a small babbling brook flowing down from a densely forested mountain. He made it his temporary haven and set up a mission there. There he met the local inhabitants the monk had told him about. Stayed for the winter and made friends with them, which, to his surprise, were indeed very small men who had no hair on their faces. Called themselves Thule. That place is now called Kirkjubaejarklaustur."

At this point, Patty's eyes opened wide, became deadly serious, and pointed an accusing finger around the table at each person, as if they were about to be found guilty of some uncommitted infraction.

"'Tis hard being at sea for long time without a woman, tough on the monks. You see, in those days, monks and priests could marry and have sex. Some of Brendan's monks began to fornicate with the local women, who were pretty loose and easy. No morals, none at all. Heathens but damn pretty. But Brendan, a pure man by God's ordination, could have no woman. He wanted purity and forced the monks to marry them. Within a year, they all had youngsters. You see, Brendan didn't know this at the time, but his hell was just a volcano erupting in Iceland."

Seeing the questioning faces of his listeners, he paused, took another drink, and continued.

"How do we know? You don't have to take my word for this, it's written in the Viking sagas. Not just one but in three of them. Vikings wrote that they found a mission with a large cross on it when they arrived in Iceland three hundred years later. Found the Irish, drove them out, and took over their settlement until they could set up their own. The Vikings even state it was Gaelic monks. Found men there who were bigger and fairer than the others. White. Had blue and brown eyes. Wrote about it too. The Vikings' legends say the robed white men had lived there for a long time but said most of the first people white settlers moved on after just one year. Recorded all this in their writing called *Papers.* Still readable today. Besides the Vikings, an Irish monk called Bicuil wrote a book *De Mensura Orbis Terrae* in 825. Read it from cover to cover."

The listeners, though now mostly drunk, marveled how Patty, who knew so many big words, could be a humble Ha Ha Bay fisherman.

"In fact, St. Brendan did move on the following spring. He was already over seventy and could not afford to waste time. Learned from the Thule people that Iceland was not their ancestral home. Some ten families had gotten lost fifty years earlier while hunting for seals on the ice floes and ended up there. Now, with St. Brendan's big ship, they all wanted to go back to their homeland, a huge island to the west they called Thule or Kalaallit Nunaat. Of course, Brendan's curraghs could not carry more than seventeen or eighteen people, so he left his married monks behind to build a monastery and civilize the Thule people. Instead, took with him six older experienced natives who knew how to navigate through the treacherous waters."

"Explain who they are now," interrupted Walter Taylor, Ha Ha Bay's oldest and most revered citizen, who had heard the story plenty of times, shaking his pipe at Patty as a stern reprimand of his mindlessness. He was one of the few in attendance considerate enough to make sure all understood. That respect was often called upon to act as community policeman to keep the more boisterous troublemakers in line.

"We now call them Eskimos or Inuit," Patty clarified obediently.

"Call them Eskimos. Ask questions if you don't know, but don't interrupt needlessly," Walter encouraged the young listeners.

"That was a smart move," Patty went on. "Brendan would soon find out that navigating in the ever-changing swift currents of the frigid North Atlantic in pompous religious regalia was not like sailing in that balmy Mediterranean pond. For two weeks, they sailed smoothly westward. Very warm. Then it hit, like Satan himself. Howling bone-chilling winds swept down from the north. For the next two weeks, they were constantly buffeted by northeasterly gales and blown far off course, becoming entrapped among the huge, dense icebergs. Nearly froze to death. The ox skins on their curragh froze and cracked. Started to leak badly. Soon they ran out of food and water."

Patty, now feeling his drinks, started to become more emotional and graphic.

"The Eskimos were filthy heathens but hardworking, tough little bastards. Brendan figured he would meet his Maker, made his peace with him, and turned control over to the senior Eskimo with instructions for their burial.

"The Eskimos found this amusing and laughed at it for days. You see, they were at home on the ice floes. It was everyday living for them, the ancestral life they loved. They knew survival in the Arctic. Thrilled to be back home again. Knew exactly where to locate seals and polar bears among the ice pans and, within a week, had killed several of each with their spears, sometimes from the curragh while still sailing. Scared of nothing, faced those polar bears single-handed. Landed on the ice and hauled the curragh upon it. Built igloos for warmth to wait out the late spring blizzards. Made fires with the seal blubber and cured the bearskins right there on the snow. Fixed the leaks on their ship by changing the ox skins with watertight sealskins, the same way they did on their kayaks. Taught Brendan and his monks how to select the choice pieces of raw meat to eat and how to drink the hot nutritious seal blood before the animal cooled. Then they sewed proper warm clothes for the monks, who would never have survived without it.

"Brendan was both impressed and puzzled how, or why, people would choose to live on moving ice sheers for weeks, even months. So eternally grateful was he that he forgave their ungodliness, blessed them all, and made them all good Catholics.

"Things steadily improved from there on. And to make a long story short, within a few more weeks, they made land on the west coast of Kalaallit Nunaat. To Brendan's surprise, it was free of ice and very warm for late June. Life had returned. Even more puzzling, there was a large settlement of Eskimos there. Some cozy summer place they called Nuuk.

"Was treated like gods by the Eskimos, and Brendan made sure they, in turn, were treated with respect. Learned from them there were different cultures on the island. One people lived inland and hunted caribou, reindeer, musk oxen, and other animals. They domesticated dogs and used them to track down animals as well as to pull their wooden sleds. A different tribe lived on the coast year-round and hunted walruses, seals, whales, and caught fish. They had large metal knifes for cutting snow and a sharp circular knife, called an *ulu*, for scraping animal hides. Were experts at hitting their targets with a harpoon at fifty yards.

"But the people from Nuuk, who were wanderers, did all these and were excellent sailors using only tiny kayaks.

"Brendan stayed in Nuuk for a year. Learned all he could about the history and lifestyle of the people. Admired their resourceful culture. Very friendly people. Liked them. Winter was harsh, but their host showed them how to survive nicely. Mastered igloo building, the use of the *ulu*, and harpoon throwing. Had to change their priestly robes to sealskin, though, for warmth. Caught, processed, and sewed it themselves. Began using polar bearskins as bedclothes while sleeping in the curragh as they explored along the coast of Kalaallit Nunaat."

"Pardon me, Patty," asked one of the young listeners, cautiously, slurring his words. "Where is this Kalit Nunit?"

"Kalaallit Nunaat! Say it properly. 'Tis their bloody country. Lived there for ten thousand years," Patty chastised sternly, now drunk. "Those depraved Vikings later called it Greenland.

"Brendan built a monastery and converted some to Christianity. Life was good. Brendan wanted to stay longer, but more of his monks were courting the young Eskimo women, and he was concerned they would desert him and remain behind. Besides, he had heard tales of the elders around their evening campfires that their ancestors came from a large land just to the west that was only ten days' paddle away in their kayaks and that some brave, foolhardy young people still undertook the journey to prove their manhood. Brendan offered to take six of them with him, but all refused, saying giant red savages lived in the south of that land, who paddled wooden boats much faster than theirs and had powerful bows and arrows.

"With the spring breakup, the monks reluctantly said good-bye to their friends and headed directly west. A fair northeasterly wind took them to the land they sought in just six days. But they were disappointed, a more desolate and bleak land they had never witnessed. Flat rocks. No trees. Just a few animals that could see you for miles. Hunting was impossible. Chilly winds constantly howling down from the north.

"Brendon did not tarry, headed south. The Promised Land he envisioned had warm, luscious green forest, flowery meadows, with multitudes of birds and bees humming night and day.

"The wind was in his favor as he hugged the coast. For more than a month, they contoured the bleak, monotonous coastline when suddenly it ended abruptly and they found themselves far out to sea again. They realized the land behind had been just another island. But by now, Brendon and his crew had warm clothes, knew how to harpoon seals, small baleen whales, and fish—which were plentiful."

"Which island was that?" asked the young lad again, fully engrossed in Patty's saga.

"Baffin Island, me b'ye. Didn't know it, but they were now heading for the Labrador. Made it too. At Godspeed. Six sunsets after that, saw God's good earth again, but it was almost as barren as they left behind. Except for a few low wind-stunted bushes. But it had high mountains, sheltered coves, and numerous small streams with lots of fish.

"Doggedly, they pushed on south, staying close to shoreline for shelter, food, and water. Gradually, the air became warmer until finally, they reached a long sandy beach at the mouth of a wide river. Went ashore and made camp in the lush, dense spruce forest. Plenty of everything. Heard wolves for the first time, saw lots of wildlife, especially caribou and moose. Discovered several abandoned, crude birch bark camps, fresh-burnt charcoal from fires, well-worn foot trails through the woods, all signs of civilization, but saw not a living soul. But at night, they kept one man as a guard, felt they were being watched.

"After a week to recuperate, give thanks to the Blessed Virgin, patch their boat, and gather food, they moved on—"

"Tell them where this place was," interrupted Walter Taylor again.

"Yes. 'Twas on the Labrador coast, at the mouth of Hamilton River. About where Rigolet is now."

It drew sighs of approval from everybody.

"But they weren't out of sight of land an hour when they noticed in the distance twenty or thirty small boats following them. They were the fast canoes Brendan had been warned about. Two or three men in each canoe. Brendan wanted to go back and welcome them, but his monks would have none of it. They had heard the horrific stories from the Eskimos of their cannibalistic ways, their fast canoes, and their skill at killing with bows and arrows. And much to Brendan's displeasure, a chase ensued. At first, the savages gained rapidly on the large curragh, and soon Brendan could clearly see they were indeed strong men who looked like giants. Scantily dressed but nonetheless neat and clean. Faces artistically painted with red and white stripes and eagle feathers in their hair. Canoes painted too. Very noisy.

"But Brendan was a seasoned sailor with a few tricks up his sleeve. He headed straightaway from the sheltered bay, directly out into the stormy North Atlantic, knowing the savages could not pursue them out of sight of the coast in their tiny, fragile, wooded boats for safety reasons. And after a brief period of bloodcurdling howling and gesturing and shooting a hail of arrows, which fell far short, the pursuers turned tail and headed back to the coast.

"This pleased the monks, who gave a sigh of relief, but Brendan was pretty upset with them. In effect, they had mutinied. Their mission was to teach the heathens their Christian values, and being sniveling cowards in the face of adversity was no way to impress brave savages. Monks were supposed to be men of an all-powerful God, who would protect them in such times of peril, and Brendan gave them a good dressing down.

"For the next six days, they sailed southeast, staying a few miles offshore, praying and watching diligently for signs of the Promised Land. Then in early July, they spotted a narrow strait with an island guarding its entrance.

"The Strait of Belle Isle?" guessed a teenage student, who was hearing the story for the first time.

"Wasn't called that then, but you're spot on," Patty responded, impressed. But that respect quickly dissipated when he realized the minor was drinking moonshine. "That stuff will stunt your growth," he chastised.

"'Twas a calm, clear day they sailed around Belle Isle. Warm too. Sun blazing down. Then they saw a mountain of dense fog approaching, so dark it looked to Brendan as if hell was to envelop him in total darkness. He had all the monks kneel and pray for redemption. But on it came like bellowing night clouds rolling down from the heavens. For three days, they lay becalmed in total darkness. Not a draft of wind, just a solid wall of bone-chilling fog. Unable to see ten feet.

"On the fourth day, it lifted, and Brendan was horrified to find his curragh surrounded by humpback whales. Sea monsters were a sailor's worst nightmare in those days. Boats were only bite-size. He then realized the fog and the whales were a premonition from the Lord warning them to stop running and set up a mission to help their enemies, or they would be swallowed up by these giant beasts as Jonah was."

Patty paused again to formulate the rest of his saga as the group fidgeted impatiently.

"Old Micmac Indian legends passed down from generation to generation say Brendan, one day, just mysteriously appeared out of the fog bank in Ha Ha Bay, pulled his boat over the neck, right here, and sailed all the way down the bottom of Pistolet Bay. Ghostly white men from the icy north with long white hair and white beards who walked unsteadily, they claim, who at night wore white bearskin clothes, sealskin boots, and floated over the water in a sealskin boat but in the daytime became red and skinny.

"Indeed this was true. It was now July and hot. Brendan's monks used their warm polar bear clothes at night and changed into their scarlet robes during the heat of the day. And months at sea can make anybody walk like an Egyptian. Met the Micmacs too. Big brawny Indians, really friendly. Showed Brendan where to find plenty of fish—especially shellfish—and wild berries. Taught the monks how to cure meat and fish by slowly smoking it over a birch wood fire until the water was gone. How to cover their skin in red ochre to keep mosquitoes away, how to build wigwams as temporarily shelters; and make fire by rubbing sticks together.

"And as luck would have it, July was the time when the Micmac tribes around Ha Ha Bay had their yearly powwow, and with so many knowledgeable chiefs, it proved an opportune time for Brendan to get the full picture. The grand chiefs smoked a tobacco pipe and passed it to Brendan, who willingly took a puff and gave it to all his monks. The grand chief explained it was their gesture of peace and friendship. Brendan likened it to the incense burned in the Catholic Church and was pleased.

"The peaceful unarmed monks made a real impression on the Micmac tribes. It was an abnormality for them to meet strangers who wanted to help. And something about them intrigued Brendan as well. They were not savages in his passive way of thinking, they actually worshipped a god called Nishkam, the Great Spirit.

"When Brendan inquired why his monks were treated with such respect, honored even, the local chief related a story foretold by Nishkam, who had once travelled across the waters and learned the hearts of the white-haired demons. Nishkam said large islands with spirits as numerous as the trees of the forests would one day float like clouds across the ocean from the east. The trees would be pale-faced people who wanted to share their land, and they should welcome them and trade with them. To fight them would be hopeless, they were so strong and smart.

"Brendan was astounded by their eerily accurate prophecy and learned all he could about their gods to determine if they lived in the Promised Land.

"Brendan was also anxious to move on and recounted his holy calling to the chief, who, in turn, told him he could travel for years, the land was so big it had no end. Said he had heard rumors from a people who lived by a large river far to the south of a beautiful tropical place with white sandy beaches, a place where no clothes was needed, fruit was plentiful all year round, with seas abounding in fish and wildlife so tame it considered humans harmless. Everything there was free for the taking. A place where a person could live off the land forever, without ever working.

"To Brendan, such an idyllic place could only be the Promised Land. It sounded precisely like the biblical Garden of Eden. Yet he was indecisive. He had already been travelling for two years and was now seventy-two. On the other hand, the hosts urged him to go before autumn, warning that the local winters were long and frigid. Even worse, there was another tribe of people on the island who called themselves Beothuks, bloodthirsty cannibals, whereas the people in the warm lands were friendly.

"Brendan took a few weeks to contemplate the idea and explore the area. On one of his forging expeditions a few days later, he found a huge blue whale stranded on a sandbar. This was an omen, the Lord's approval for him to continue his divine voyage. He recalled during the hectic voyage how he had been unable able to land and erect a cross to celebrate Easter. So he ordered all eleven monks to climb onto the whale's back and held Easter mass right there and then to praise God's mastery over such monstrous sea creatures, especially the murderous kraken.

"Grateful for their hospitality, Brendan set up a makeshift cross from a piece of whitewashed driftwood near Milan Arm and blessed them. Made the local Micmac elder a monk and sanctioned him with the task to lead his mission.

"In early August, after provisioning his curragh and holding mass with the Micmacs, the monks sailed reluctantly south through the strait. And for the next twenty days, they followed the coast of the island. Not too warm but comfortable. Perfect sailing. Stopped occasionally for water and food. Fish plentiful. Lived good.

"Then without warning, they were again miles from shore heading into the unknown. Five days they sailed before spotting land again."

Patty paused for a time and took a deep breath and to savor a slug of moonshine. His audience waited eagerly.

"Well? Tell us what happened," queried the lad, now drunk and becoming belligerent.

"Mind your prate now," warned Walter Taylor. "Patty is just taking a breather."

"For some reason," Patty recommenced, "the next three years of Brendan's travel was not written down. It appears that in that time he travelled all the way down to what is now Chesapeake Bay. And Brendan's monks must have been busy. What we know are yarns from those explorers and settlers who came later. The Vikings, the Spanish, and the English all said that from Maine to Florida, they occasionally met fair-skinned natives with light hair and blue eyes, who related chronicles of their pale-faced ancestors from over the water and who showed them how to make metal from bog ore.

"In the pope's paper, *Navigatio Sancti Brendani,* it appears Brendan did find his version of heaven in what is now West Virginia. In paradise, the group of monks travelled for forty days inland amid the torrid heat and moisture encountering numerous animals of all sizes, shapes, and colors. A modern day Noah's ark. Most were relatively tame, but snakes concerned Brendan the most. They were devils who crawled on the ground that could cast spills and appear in different forms. Shape-shifters who had temped Adam and Eve. Brendan recalled how St. Patty drove the snakes out of his homeland. He wondered if he had the power do the same in the new endless land. But to his dismay, he held no such power.

"Their Indian guide led them to a deep, fast-flowing, muddy river about a mile wide, which they reached on Christmas Day. Unable to cross, they built a mission near a large rock. Using ogham, the official Irish writing of the religious educated elite, he described a complete record of Christ's nativity for all the natives to see."

Patty paused to get several new bottles of moonshine and passed them around the table.

"Tell them what river that was," ordered Walter Taylor, lighting his pipe, always cognizant of the education of the community's young people. Wanted all Ha Ha Bay legends to be passed on.

Patty, who never smoked, claiming it was bad for his health, took a huge chug of moonshine and continued.

"Somewhere in the upper part of the mighty Mississippi. Brendan lived there among the peaceful Shawnee Indians in his Promised Land until he was seventy-five. But he wanted to die in his native Ireland, and legend says he returned home by the same route."

"Tell us about the voyage back," insisted the teenager, disappointed at the abrupt ending.

"Can't tell you what's not written down, my lad, can't make it up."

"That's fiction!" challenged the drunken lad.

"Fiction? Not according to the holy Catholic church. Brendan did return to Rome, and as promised, the pope gave him his most esteemed scribe, who wrote the details of his travels. Made him a saint, right there and then. Cross my heart. Read it myself in the *Navigatio Sancti Brendani* in the Vatican. Hundreds of copies in a dozen different languages."

"Can't be done," the lad reiterated defiantly, now drunk, attempting to bait Patty for an argument.

"Been to his gravesite in Annaghdown. Died in 577. Lived a long life, ninety-three years," mused Patty pensively, dismissing the lad.

"No one lived ninety-three years in those days," retorted the lad.

"My son, there is no romance in your soul," answered Patty calmly, passing around more moonshine, bypassing him. "Learn to read the writings of the great ones."

"Yes, truth is stranger than fiction," pondered Walter Taylor, coming to Patty's aid. Turning to the lad and shaking his pipe, he lectured, "Those who can, do, those who can't, criticize. Now that's enough of your sassiness, get out of here."

"Can't be done," the lad whispered defiantly under his breath as he staggered obediently away from the table.

But in 1976, Tim Severin, a British navigator, proved that it could be done. He sailed from the exact location Brendon did fifteen hundred years earlier, in a boat that he had constructed using the precise details described by Brendan in the *Navigatio Sancti Brendani.* Followed the exact same route as Brendan, wintered in the north, and reached Newfoundland the next summer.

As in Patty's tale, the Vikings left detailed accounts in three separate sagas of meeting people who knew of the Irish monks and even spoke their language, which they understood. This is clearly stated in their written saga called *Papers.* They called the land south of Vinland—the present day L'Anse aux Meadows, Newfoundland—*Lvitramammaland*, meaning Land of the White Men, and the area around Chesapeake Bay they called *Irland ed mikla*, which is Greater Ireland.

What's more, Barry Fell, a Harvard marine biologist, in 1983 happened upon petroglyphs, which were of the Irish ogham alphabet in origin, chiseled into solid rocks near the Ohio River in West Virginia. The writings detailed the virgin birth of Jesus. The river is a forty-day walk from the seashore of Chesapeake Bay.

In addition, the National Museum in Nuuk, Kalaallit Nunaat, displays comprehensive exhibitions of the Irish culture.

Truth is indeed stranger than fiction.

Chronicle 14

The Legend of Henri Boucher

The only way to die is to go out in a blaze of glory.

Fueled by pietistic, fanatical, religious denominations such as the Methodists, the eighteenth amendment to the United States Constitution was ratified on January 16, 1919, prohibiting the manufacture, sale, and importation of liquor, but went ignored for a full year due to nearly universal opposition. However, when its provisions began to be enforced on January 17, 1920, it touched of a nationwide backlash by the common man whose only respite from the monotony of endless labor was a social drink, initiating one of the greatest social upheavals in American history and destroying the very social fabric the religious fanatics wished to preserve.

Some Canadian provinces such as Nova Scotia and New Brunswick and the Dominion of Newfoundland soon followed suit.

In record time, millions of clandestine operations sprung up in basements and hideaways to serve the thirsty public. New York alone had more than one hundred thousand. These illegal operations became known as *speakeasies*, and millions of common citizens became criminals practically overnight.

The Bouchers of Nova Scotia were an enterprising bunch of kindhearted, home-styled scalawags, who were generally accepted as good, honest, god-fearing Christian folks by whomever made their acquaintances. They were descendants of Métis who moved from the French Shore of Newfoundland a century ago. As with most rational, reasoning people in the 1920s, their homespun religious interpretation of Prohibition dictated their logical response that if illegal activity caused no physical harm and was perpetrated for the collective benefit of the masses, it was not considered a crime per se, more like an ill-devised political law. In fact, history would prove them right, but it would come at a terrible cost.

Rum-running during the Prohibition years from St. Pierre and Miquelon to the United States, Canada, and Newfoundland was at epidemic proportions, The specter of exorbitant profits lured hundreds of honest people in small open inshore fishing boats to venture into the stormy seas off Newfoundland, and with ocean fog as a perfect shroud 167 days of the year on the Grand Banks and with only a few patrol boats covering tens of thousands of square miles of ocean, the success rate was usually good, better than 90 percent.

The Bouchers were also good friends; all six brothers toiled harmoniously together. Even their wives and large families cooperated abnormally well, jelled by their respected position in the community and their faith in the local Catholic Church. In fact, all the residents of the little community of Rocky Head in Nova Scotia were of the same mentality. Every person in the little hamlet knew the Bouchers were champion rumrunners to the United States, praised their entrepreneurial spirit, and reaped the benefits of their successes.

But most recognition went to Pere Henri—the Old Man as he was affectionately known—the patriarch of the clan, who was uncharacteristically intelligent for a *poor* fisherman. He was an avid reader who loved the heroic, romantic, salty tales of roaming pirates and, in his own mind, considered himself a true bloodthirsty scalawag. However, reality could not be further from the truth.

Ten years earlier, he had purchased an old fishing schooner, some predicted a derelict coffin, from a widowed woman in Lunenburg whose husband supposedly drowned at sea along with his entire crew. The ship had been found drifting with nobody aboard, and it was assumed the crew was all at sea in dories attending their trawls and nets when a northeaster hit, as no fishing gear was found on the ship.

But Henri grasped the hidden meaning. The ship was painted grey completely. The sails were grey and shallow. It had a deceptive name for a Nova Scotia fishing boat, *Newfie Cod*. It had an unusually wide beam yet an extremely low-profiled hull, designed to float low in the water. Henri recognized it as a ghost ship from his storybooks, a fast runner known as a member of the banana fleet. He quickly traded his farm for the old ship to become a rich fisherman.

At least that's what he convinced his wife and family at the time, and he actually did fish for a couple of years, to learn the finer points of the art of sailing and to teach his family to be sailors. But his intentions were far more sinister. He knew he could make more profit delivering a single load of rum to the Americans in the Boston States than could be made in five years of fishing. His wife, whose ancestors were from Ha Ha Bay, Newfoundland, was acutely aware of the vagrancies of fishing, grasped his intentions, and secretly supported him all the way.

And run rum they did. Within eight years, they were known far and wide for their daring exploits and innovative techniques in outsailing the motorized cutters of both the Canadian and American coast guards. With a French background giving them the ability to speak the language fluently to communicate with their suppliers in St. Pierre and Miquelon, the Bouchers quickly gained the inside advantage and soon had their suppliers giving them volume discounts. Within a few years, with their reputation for success, they had their rum-run lines in place, a reliable, shadowy network of contacts embedded all up and down the shoreline among the hidden bays and coves en route to all the major destinations, with secret, sophisticated signaling codes at the rendezvous points with instructions where to toss the barrels of rum overboard. Their fame had attained hero worship with distributors to the speakeasies. Some say the Old Man knew Al Capone personally. And the community of Rock Head was soon rechristened Boucherville in their honor and prospered right along with them.

July 13, 1922, dawned with a gentle breeze from the east and a cold grey dense fog, ideal weather for clandestine operations. The Bouchers had always kept their *fishing* schooner provisioned for such eventualities. With the fishing season in full swing, the government revenuers would not suspect anything illegal, even more so now since the prestigious Catholic Church had recently given the clan glowing character referencess at church services as God's role model for functioning agreeably together and sharing everything equally with the community, often going for weeks to Ha Ha Bay, Newfoundland, to get a early start on the cod fishery. Of course, the church received the most generous donations of all.

The revenuer's stool pigeons watched surreptitiously from their hilltop hideaway as Henri, the Acadian Kingpin, as the authorities labeled him, his six sons, and four of his grandsons stood on the deck of the *Newfie Cod* with its fishing gear overflowing its railing head out the narrow harbor entrance toward Newfoundland.

The Bouchers knew they were being monitored but considered them small-fry, minor nuisances; a small bribe would silence them later, parasites whose only interest was a share of the spoils. In short, it was just another normal beginning.

Sailing in dense fog was a dangerous proposition in the sea lanes with the new larger faster-moving motorized steam vessels, but Henri, as always, when opportunity presented itself, threw caution to the wind, headed directly for St. Pierre. And as always, within five days, he was fully loaded with barrels of rum, whiskey, and champagne, waiting for a foggy day. But this time, it was a bit slower. He had a premonition of disaster. He was fidgety and anxious to sail. That night, he changed the name of the ship to the *Gloucester Fisherman,* just in case, and covered his decks with fishing nets.

Next day, it being still bright and sunny, he sailed a mile or so offshore and fished for cod, as it would fill his idle time, while securing early the fish that he usually salted away for the winter. Fish was plentiful, and within two days, he had all he could fit into his schooner. He was actually a bit too low in the water for fast sailing. He went back to port to wait out the calm and sunshine. A dense fog and a stiff southwesterly breeze would be needed for the American run.

Tarrying too long in a busy port would cause suspicion or recognition and, even worse, breed contempt. The ship's name would also have to be changed several times. Scalawags were always willing to turn you in for a few dollars or as a plea bargain for a lighter sentence for some friend in prison. Henri knew all too well there was so such thing as honor among the thieves. But two extra days in port was seldom a problem. Three was his limit. He felt relatively safe for the time being.

Unknown to Henri, suspicious shadows were lurking. His problem would come indirectly from an unexpected source—his faithful longtime friend, Jacques, his order clerk and drinking partner, who had a loose tongue when drunk, which, of late, was often. Henri, who always stayed at his friend's home when in port, uncharacteristically mentioned his new selected route to New York the next day.

Next day brought success, dense fog, wind, and rain. Henri was at sea from the crack of dawn and, six hours later, was sailing speedily along with a stiff breeze in his quarter, when to his surprise, out the fog a Canadian Preventive Services' cutter appeared, firing a warning shot across his bow. Henry was stunned; he was in international waters and without as much as a hail. The world-recognized marine limit was twelve miles, and stopping someone on the high seas, except for help or during wartime, was piracy.

Then it hit him like a flash of St. Elmo's fire.

If there were anything worse than the atrocious North Atlantic's weather or the meddling coast guard, it was privateers. True bloodthirsty pirates! They were not content to simply steal the stash and release the ship; they summarily slaughtered the crew, sunk the ship, or set it on fire. They covered their tracks completely. For the first time in ten years, the pirate wannabe had come face-to-face with the grim reality of his storybooks. Unable to outrun the cutter with his excessive load, he knew the ending would be just as gruesome as the written words. The same fate as the original owners of the ship awaited them.

For years, everyone on board had practiced firing firearms into the air as a diversion, how to dump oil or whiskey on the water and set it alight, how to throw up a smoke screen using sealing pitch to confuse the authorities, or dropping fishing gear in the cutters' path to ensnare their propellers. Those techniques normally dissuaded the authorities, who themselves were not enthusiastic about Prohibition. But privateers were not civilized people. Henri knew that none of these tactics were any match for the recklessness of the pirates, who would use the cannons on the cutter, which was most likely stolen and its crew murdered. The result was life or death. Now was the true acid test.

Being old, Henri knew his time was up. He calmly explained their grave situation to his crew and asked for three martyrs. They all volunteered, so he picked the two oldest sons and left stern directives for the others to obey. Splitting up the remaining crew into three dories, each with a senior member as captain, he ordered them to row in three different directions—one group to Newfoundland, another to Nova Scotia, and one back to St. Pierre. There was no time for mushy good-byes, just three Hail Marys.

Henri and his two older sons decided to directly confront the cutter, which was faster but smaller. His intent was to provide enough time for the three rowboats to become lost in the fog. He quickly set fire to the ship to feign destroying its cargo and prepared to go down fighting, knowing the privateers would not allow the schooner to burn to the waterline until they had possession of the contraband, and it would take some time for them to extinguish the flames.

A brief, fierce, one-sided firefight soon ensued with rifles. Old Henri, reverting back to his storybook tales, found the atmosphere bizarre but exciting; there was an eerie orange glow emanating from the thick smoke and flame, intermingling with the dense fog and being carried aloft by the wind, as if it were the trail of the new airplanes. Inspired, Henri, true to his legend, having no intention to see his sons tortured, decided to go out in the blaze of glory he had always dreamed of. Awaiting his chance, he quickly swung his schooner directly across the bow of the cutter.

Just then, fate intervened. A fast modern freighter, *Norwegian Atlantic,* appeared out of the mist, plowing directly into the midsection of the cutter, slicing it in half. The cutter, in turn, slammed into the fully laden *Newfie Cod*, causing it to explode in a huge fireball, spreading smoke and fire over a large stretch of sea, and showering debris onto the deck of the freighter. The freighter reversed engines and attempted to stop to rescue the sailors. But the sea was awash with debris. Barrels of rum and whiskey were floating amid the flames and exploding. Codfish covered the sea like a blanket. The smell of gas and alcohol was stifling; the freighter was forced to move a safe distance away. By the time the flames abated, the wind had increased to gale force and the fog had become denser. Maneuvering around the fishing nets could cause propeller entanglement. The best the freighter could do was send an SOS message for help, explaining it had collided with a cutter from Canadian Preventive Services, slicing it in half, and all the people aboard were believed dead, then detailing how the cutter in turn had collided with a privateer rum-running ship called the *Gloucester*

Fisherman that they apparently had captured, causing it to explode, and its crew was thought to be lost as well.

By the time the storm had abated two days later and an armada of research vessels had converged on the area, all survivors and debris had been dispersed; nothing was ever found.

In a long drawn-out inquiry three months later into the loss of the Canadian Preventive Services cutter, it was revealed that no such ship named the *Gloucester Fisherman* was registered in Canada, the United States, or Newfoundland, and it was assumed the schooner to be the *Newfie Cod,* as the Bouchers had reported their schooner lost at sea two months earlier and had applied for the insurance money. The captain of the *Norwegian Atlantic* testified that the floating grey-colored debris from the explosion matched the court description of the *Newfie Cod.* The survivors from the dories of the *Newfie Cod* were thus summoned to court.

The Boucher relatives were repeatedly examined and cross-examined at the hearing but stuck together, reiterating that they had escaped in dories from the *Newfie Cod* after it was captured by pirates on the cutter, who had killed their father and two brothers, and that their dories had become separated in the fog and heavy gale. They detailed how their father and brothers fought off the privateers as long as possible for them to escape and that the cutter was loaded with contraband liquor, not their fishing schooner, which was low in the water with a full load of fresh cod, some of which was had not been cured, leaving them slow and unmaneuverable when attacked. The captain of the freighter gave credibility to their story by confirming that there was a huge mass of fish, as well as fishing buoys intertwined with its nets, floating on the water after the accident.

The Bouchers related heroic tales on how their dories had become separated in the fog and heavy gale, how one crippled back to St. Pierre the next day leaking like a sieve, how a second took a week to make it to Nova Scotia without food or water, while a third was picked up by a fishing boat out of Burin, Newfoundland. The rescuers of the latter two dories testified they found its crew suffering from thirst, starvation, and exposure, indicating a fast escape.

However, the fly in the ointment was Henri's friend, Jacques, who testified he had sold the liquor to him and that the *Newfie Cod* was headed for speakeasy distributers in New York. He even produced the bill of lading. But in this, he lost credibility; bootleggers kept no record.

As the days dragged laboriously on, the inquiry became progressively more negative for the Bouchers, and they were about to be found responsible for the loss and, as such, relegated to the level of pirates, when it took a decisive turn for the positive. Father Bauer of Boucherville mysteriously appeared dressed in his impressive religious regalia and presented an emotional oration on the benevolence of Henri Boucher, such that if St. Peter himself had not been previously selected as the cornerstone of the Catholic Church, Henri would have been the superior candidate.

The panel, henceforth, sheepishly reversed their stance and concluded that the *Newfie Cod* had indeed faced down the commandeered cutter, and Henri was pronounced an honorable citizen, a true seafaring folk hero. It was also recommended he be immortalized with statues to be erected in both Gloucester and Halifax. As a closing statement, a eulogy by the *Norwegian Atlantic's* captain deemed that "Henri and his sons were indeed honest ethical citizens, who truly went out in a blaze of glory."

The panel titled their report "The Legend of Henri Boucher."

Henri would have found that amusing and would have chastised them by saying that he was neither an angel nor a devil, just an average man who simply fought a bad law and died as any father would, saving his family.

But the true legend of the Old Man lives on to this day in numerous tales, poems, and pictures in the drinking bars and gambling parlors that were once speakeasies where his exploits had been celebrated in their true perspective, that he had far surpassed the fabled fictional pirate stories of his childhood fairy tales and that his elusive tactics were instrumental in changing the alcohol prohibition policies of several nations.

By 1929, the United States, parts of Canada, and Newfoundland all agreed Prohibition was an unenforceable law and conceded that it had caused freedom to be lost on a massive scale. Facing an international revolution, the United States introduced the Twenty-first

Amendment to its constitution to repeal the Prohibition law. It was ratified on December 5, 1933, and was the wettest Christmas ever. Other countries soon followed.

Still, the religious fanatics did not admit defeat. They called the *Volstead Act*, their popular name for the eighteenth amendment, their *Noble Experiment* and blamed its failure on Satan.

Chronicle 15

The Princess of Terra Nova

The British like the Spanish before them will have affixed to their character the indelible reproach of having extirpated a whole race of people.
—Magistrate John Bland, 1792

Of all the tragic stories ever told in Ha Ha Bay or throughout Newfoundland's history, none is more heart-wrenching, or inhumane, than the reprehensible demise of the Newfoundland's First Nations' people, the Beothuks. An ethnic cleansing endorsed by both civil and official government policy alike and perpetrated by nearly every civilized European nation and on such an unprecedented scale that even today we strive in vain to come to grips with our carnal nature. We make irrational justifications that in some bizarre, unexplained way, it wasn't our fault—they were equally as evil; that it was just the natural evolution of history; that it was the result of the island's unique ecology; that they were the ignorant victims of a free market enlightened economy; that it was merely survival of the fittest; that they could have chosen to move off the island, and some argue they did; that by not discussing it, the guilt remains hidden or is less painful; or that it wasn't us, it was our ancestors, our mentality isn't like that today. The lists of excuses and condescending platitudes are endless. But in spite of our perceived piety, the stark truth remains—we committed genocide.

Be it the Vikings slaughtering *Skrælings* at Vinland in the year 1000 CE, the Genoese Giovanni Caboto in 1947 capturing "three uncivilized, ferocious and bloodthirsty natives" to take back to England to authenticate his discovery, the Portuguese explorer Gaspar Corte-Real capturing "fifty-seven strong, well-proportioned, red savages" in 1501 to take back to Europe as slaves, the French fur trappers shooting "Red Indians down like deer" for target practice in 1774, or the English fishermen blocking the "redskins'" traditional food source on the coast in 1823, historical records stand unceremoniously as stark testimony to the fact that the white man deliberately, systematically, and callously liquidated a whole race of people.

Of the two thousand strong, proud Beothuk race that inhabited every bay and cove around the rugged coast of Newfoundland when European's first arrived, by 1820, only a sick, starving, bedraggled band of seventy-two souls existed, eking out a subsistence living, cowering like frightened puppies into the wilderness around the now aptly named Red Indian Lake, occasionally running the gauntlet of fisherman's and trapper's bullets while making mad dashes down the Exploits River to Notre Dame Bay to collect a few morsels of food. Those lucky enough not to be shot later died of starvation or white man's diseases.

April 1823

Sick, cold, and hungry, Shawnadithit knew as she struggled alone through the frigid, stormy April night in 1823 to voluntarily surrender to the white fishermen on the coast of Notre Dame Bay—the same people who had so mercilessly murdered all her tribe. She would soon be departing for the spirit world to be united with her relatives who dwelt in the great *mamateek* in the sky, and like most of them, she too was suffering from the cough demon.

Contrary to what all her young life's experiences dictated, she was convinced there were still some good-spirit people left on Great Mother Earth, and she would be fortunate enough to stumble unto one. This was her real life vision quest. In her delirium, she dreamed their hearts would be compassionate and forgiving and not shoot her but have her transferred to local authorities to be sent to St. John's to collect their "Red Indian savage" bounty. There she would be prodded and studied by a few curious famous people or be forced to go to Europe to be exhibited in a zoo like an animal for entertainment; life would be hard and humiliating, but she would be warm and fed.

But more tragically, she was grieving; she had just buried her mother and sister and knew full well that she was the last person of her race left alive on the earth, and every other human being alive was her enemy.

September 1800

It was a warm brilliant starlit night with a full moon in the early autumn of 1800 as the great shaman chanted and danced alone around the lodge pole at the Beothuk temporary summer wigwam on the shores of the Great Lake (Red Indian Lake), where Doodebewshet was in labor with her second child. All seventy-one relatives of her tribe were squatted around a huge fire outside the manger, silently awaiting the blessed event.

Time was precious. It was the end of summer, and there was insufficient food for winter. While fishing near the salt water in Exploits Bay, they had been attacked and were lucky to escape with only three deaths from the white man firearms. They hoped the winter spirits would supply plenty of caribou and deer.

Soon a baby's first earthly cry rang out, but the group maintained a nervous silence. The shaman stopped and cautiously smiled with satisfaction. No one expected miracles; the mortality rate among newborns was high. But when the midwife appeared carrying a baby wrapped in a soft mink blanket, held it high, and pronounced both mother and baby were fine, instantly, the tribe exploded into cheers, dancing and whooping. A baby girl had been born. One more cherished child to replenish a vanishing breed. Seventy-two Beothuks now remained. It was good reason to thank the Great Spirit, even if it were amid disaster.

However, the celebration soon fell deathly silent as the whole tribe stared skyward in shock and awe as a long-tailed comet mysteriously appeared, sparkled brightly, flashed swiftly across the sky, disappearing into the north, the direction of the white devil's settlements. Everyone gasped in disbelief. The newborn was a bad omen, a harbinger of evil.

It would have to be drowned. All eyes instantly shifted to the shaman; magic and sorcery was his domain, not the stars. They nervously awaited his macabre instructions.

The colorfully decorated, stern-faced shaman grudgingly took a huge drink of the strong magic potion from a sealskin flask he carried on his belt. Slowly, from his leather nunny bag, he reverently retrieved his ancestral relics, chanted a sacred mantra while prancing about the towering bonfire requesting their ancient wisdom, then abruptly tossing them unto the dirt. Instantly, his face glowed with delight, his mouth agape; he seemed to stop breathing. He folded his hands and gave an unexpected bow. His audience stood up in anticipation of his tragic answer. Beaming with pride, he retrieved one special object from the ground, raised it high, and announced triumphantly to his tribe that the sky spirit wasn't a premonition of evil but the heralding of a great person being born, one who would be the most notable of all her people.

Her people were stunned. How could this be? The baby was just a girl!

Nonetheless, according to the tribe's naming ceremony in thanking the Great Spirit of Mother Earth, the shaman dabbed red ochre on her forehead and named her Shawnadithit. Festivities erupted into a night of singing and dancing.

All Shawnadithit's knowledge about her first five years of life was communicated to her by her sister (later to be rechristened as Easter Eve), four years older, who patiently cared for her well-being. They were literally two peas in a pod. Easter Eve's playtime was minimal as there were always chores to be done or they were continually on the move. Shawnadithit substituted as her real live doll and shielded her from some of the hard labor assigned to children. Although heavy, she carried her in a bearskin pouch on her back or in the hood of her caribou-skin parka.

Being hunter-gatherers, their life was in perfect tune with the cycle of the seasons and nature's food chain. Each spring, all the tribe congregated, held a grand departure feast, separated into small bands, and journeyed hundreds of miles down to the coast. First, the men travelled downriver in their heavily laden canoes to build temporary shelters, to hunt seals before the arctic ice floes moved offshore, and, if lucky, kill a whale. The foolhardy braves sometimes even paddled fifty miles offshore to the Funk Islands in canoes in heavy fog to collect a boatload of eggs; with the occasional tragedy.

Women and the remainder of the band later trekked over the marshy barrens after the snow melted. There on the seashore, for four months, they caught and cured food for the winter and enjoyed the abundant shellfish. It was the rebirth after a cold, hungry winter.

Summers were the happiest time for Shawnadithit and Easter Eve. They loved to race barefoot along the sandy beaches, watch crabs, dig clams, collect mussels, whelks, and other shellfish in the shallow water. They found the thrill of catching lobsters particularly adventuresome; they were big, hid under rocks, and fought back. Dried lobster tails was their chosen winter food and bird's eggs their summer specialty.

Even though the women were often left abandoned to do the bulk of the work, sometimes at night, if it were a safe, secluded area, they were allowed to make small bonfires from driftwood on the beach and roast their catch, sing songs, or listen to the elders spin tales of past heroic deeds.

Shawnadithit did not enjoy the courageous deeds of her elders; they always glorified killing. Many times, she had heard the heartbreaking story of her aunt Oubee who fourteen years earlier as a young girl had been kidnapped and was forced to work as a slave for the *buggishaman* (white man) on an island for two years before being taken across the ocean in a big ship, never to be seen again. Eight members of her tribe had died in that surprise raid; they had shown up loaded with animal pelts, naively believing the fishermen were friendly and wanted to trade.

She also learned that all the white devils who came from across the waters in big ships were not all from the same tribe or land, and they too fought and killed each other. The people from the land called England hated the people from the land called France, who spoke a different language, and there were many countries with people as numerous as the stars in the sky. She heard how the French traded guns for furs with the *Shannoks* (Micmacs)—their former allies—and paid them a bounty to kill the Beothuks, who refused guns because they killed animals just to sell their skins, and that destroyed Mother Nature's food chain.

One tale was particularly gruesome. Many years earlier, all the Beothuk tribes had paddled to a large point of land (Savage Cove) and had congregated for a war council when Algonquin warriors from across the narrow waters (Strait of Belle Isle) appeared in white devils' boats with guns. And even though the Beothuks fought bravely and killed many of them, they could not escape. All four hundred were slaughtered and their heads displayed on pikes in a victory ceremony. The women were then left behind to struggle to raise their families, with many dying from exhaustion and hunger.

But of all the English white devil's families that came to the coast and settled at the mouth of the Great River (Exploits River) of their tribal homeland (From Red Indian Lake to Notre Dame Bay), for as long as anybody in the tribe could remember, one was an evil spirit and feared by Beothuks and Micmacs alike. John Peyton Sr. was a white man's chief, justice of the peace, a fish and fur merchant, who every year after the summer fishing season ended journeyed inland to hunt not only animals but also Beothuks, whereas most white people would only kill if they accidently met or simply fire their guns just to scare them away. It was rumored that John Peyton Sr. was even considered a devil by the white man and was known as the butcher of the Beothuks. His son, John Peyton Jr., though less savage, still hunted Beothuks occasionally for bounty money.

It seemed to Shawnadithit that everyone hated the Beothuk and wanted their food and land. What she could not understand, since there were so few Beothuks and such a big land, why they all could not share, but she was always too afraid to ask her chief. She felt the Beothuk men were equally as warlike as the white man; they spent a lot of valuable time holding war councils on how to kill instead of how to negotiate peace, while women did all the work and suffered the most.

Easter Eve taught Shawnadithit all her survival skills, including how to swim in the shallow lagoons, but Shawnadithit's favorite pastime was drawing pictures of different birds and fish on the sandy beaches. Such diverse species of wildlife fascinated her. However, this was discouraged by the elders since it revealed their location to their enemies.

Easter Eve was more interested in sewing clothes for herself with fancy ornaments or learning to prepare meals. But most of all, the weather was warm, and they had plenty of food. However, she always had to be vigilant; she was her sister's keeper. In fact, every member of her tribe had been indoctrinated since childhood to raise the alarm should strangers appear, and an escape route was planned in advance. In such cases, it would inevitably be sheer panic to get out of range of the guns, and everything they owned would be sacrificed. Such an occurrence was expected at least once a summer, and a portion of their cured food was often buried miles inland for safekeeping.

Mosquitoes and fleas were only minor distraction since a little extra red ochre mixed with caribou grease usually solved the problem.

In the fall, they trekked back to their more permanent mamateeks on the Great Lake, dragging their heavy loads of foods on sleds behind them, or paddled upriver in their canoes laden with food for the winter. Those that traveled over the marshes collected different species of berries or herbs for medicine in sealskin bags.

It was a dangerous time; travel was slow, and they were exposed to the enemies on the open barrens. The chief and his strongest braves, armed with bows and arrows and spears, scouted ahead to search for any rogue fur trappers who may have appeared early and occupied their campsite or worse, burnt it in their absence. Since the Micmac women often married the white man, they knew the area well and acted as their scouts.

Shawnadithit and her family lived with her aunt and three uncles in the tribe's most decorated winter mamateek. Being rectangular, it was much larger than the other conical birch bark wigwams on the site. It had added layers of bark and moss for warmth and was designed to adequately accommodate several families. Two carved doorposts decorated with animal heads, feathers, and shells signified that her grandfather was a respected chief.

Her gentle uncle Longnon had a young family, and she had friends to play with on stormy nights during the long winter. Her aunt, Demasduit, who was four years older, was very kind to her but was mostly busy as she had to care for her grandmother, who had a crippled foot from stepping into a furrier's leg-hold bear trap. Her grandmother also had rheumatism in her joints, and Demasduit spent a lot time toiling in the healing sweat lodge collecting wood, making fires, pouring water on the hot rocks to make steam, and later wrapping her grandmother in large bearskin blankets as therapy. The clan took good care of each other, but still they did not feel happy; they were always scared.

One night, Shawnadithit, after eating a big meal of roasted goose, had a sacred vision in which a kind white man told her there were good spirits among them. She told her best friend Demasduit, who went ballistic, warning her not to tell anybody, as the chief was bound by tribal law to kill sympathizers. She didn't, but she still believed it.

Her grandmother once told her that in the old days, the Beothuks had conducted "silent barter" with the white man. They would leave animal skins at a disclosed location, return a few weeks later, and collect the items the white man chose to leave. Some white men were honest and left knives, axes, fishhooks, and ropes, but most left filthy clothes, mirrors, beads, and many other useless items. The silent exchange ended when they learned the clothes were often contaminated with their foreign diseases, and sometimes, they hid nearby and ambushed the Beothuks as they returned to collect their exchange. Scarlet fever, chicken pox, and the most deadly of all, consumption (tuberculosis)—the cough demon—was transmitted this way, and with their communal-style living and sweat lodge healing cycles, it had spread like wildfire until everyone was infected.

By the time Shawnadithit reached seven, she could empathize with the perils and miseries of her people and was experienced in avoiding, eluding, or escaping the white devils and their many tracking dogs. She had witnessed two of her band members shot in the back, three dying after being trampled by stampeding caribou in the deer fences; another two had frozen to death, and one boy her age starved to death after getting lost on his vision quest.

But she did not believe she was just another forest animal with a *kill-or-be-killed mentality* like her elders preached. Some white people never troubled them, at times even waving and smiling when they accidently passed, but such instances were rare.

For as long as Shawnadithit could remember, she had suffered the terrible pangs of hunger. One fall day after she turned eight, she felt really happy; her band had just killed seven caribou for the winter. She contentedly spent the full day alone at the lakeshore, engrossed in washing the meat in the chilly water, as other women toiled equally hard preparing, smoking, and storing it before it spoiled. She was also conscious that her precarious position at the river in full view of passing canoes was dangerous and that, as a young girl, she could be easily captured. But she dreamed if she were captured, it would be by her good-spirit person who would treat her kindly and make her a famous Beothuk princess.

Without warning, a shot rang out. There was a painful sting in her right leg. She jumped up to escape but collapsed to the ground. She gave a series of ear-splitting shrieks to warn her relatives then, crying and desperate, hastily dragged herself across the sandy beach, up through the prickly gooseberry bushes, scraping the skin from one knee. Hiding behind a large fallen tree, she placed her hand over her mouth to stifle her choking sobs from the unbearable pain.

From her perch, she could see the bearded white devils' boat, piled high in the centre with animal skins, heading downriver. Though young, she realized the two men inside were the French fur traders who married Micmacs and who hated the Beothuks for raiding their traplines. But more troubling was that she was now abandoned; all her relatives had scattered. That was the code; a life was expendable for the greater good of the tribe.

The trappers aimlessly fired a few more shots in her direction and continued downriver. Thankful she was only their target practice, she inspected her wounds and found there were just three tiny holes in the back of her leg with little bleeding. In agonizing pain, she meticulously covered them and her skinned knee with myrrh from a fir tree, retied her leggings, and began to struggle back to her mamateek, about a hundred feet inland, hidden behind tall trees for shelter, knowing full well she might be alone for a week and die from lead poisoning.

Shawnadithit was astounded to see her sister and grandmother, who, after having heard the gunshots, disobeyed the chief's directive and remained behind to help her, knowing they could be severely punished. Her grandmother, the tribe's best, and now the only doctor, wasted no time stripping her and inspecting the wounds. Ordering her sister to hold her down, her grandmother took a stone knife and painstakingly dug the three lead pellets from her leg as she screamed hysterically. A turpentine poultice was placed on her wounds to draw out the poison then overlaid with birch bark. Strong medicine was forced down her throat, and she was placed in a bearskin blanket near the fire. By the time the rest of the tribe crept back later that night, the emergency was over, and life continued as before.

But Shawnadithit's lack of attentiveness and foolish daydreaming of good-spirit white people was a valuable lesson she would not forget.

One of Shawnadithit's goriest and unforgettable memories occurred when she was eleven. She was about to unceremoniously witness what she has already suspected, that her people were just as cruel and callous as the white man.

Newfoundland's governor, John Duckworth, hearing the tragic stories of the slaughter of the Red Indians, organized an expedition to locate them to make a professional assessment. Winter was the best time to make such contact since the Beothuk would be embedded in permanent campsites with all the tribe nearby for security. In addition, in deep snow, they could be easily apprehended as their mobility was limited on snowshoes and would surrender without a struggle if surrounded by soldiers with fast dog teams.

In the winter of 1811, the governor sent Lt. David Buchan, a Scottish naval officer and Arctic explorer who had attempted to reach the North Pole with Franklin and who had experience in communicating with the Indians and Eskimos of the north, up the Exploits River on a peace expedition. Buchan was sympathetic to the plight of oppressed peoples and had handpicked his force of armed marines to ensure they were well disciplined and controllable. No local fishermen were permitted, wanting no confrontation with the Beothuks.

After a week of travel overland, Buchan set up his depot on the south end of Red Indian Lake and unloaded his supplies, which included many gifts of practical utensils for the Beothuks. As a quick preliminary exploratory mission, he took a few of his marines and set out to secretly determine their location and numbers, believing their encampment was further up the lake. To prevent bloodshed, his intention was to openly approach them unarmed in the daylight and welcome them personally while having his few hidden marines watching from a distance. He didn't want a display of force to terrorize them.

But fate intervened.

Unintentionally, late in the evening on the first day out, he accidently stumbled upon the whole Beothuk campsite, to the surprise of both parties. Seeing the armed marines with dogs, the Beothuks became paralyzed with fear, held up their hands, and surrendered en masse. Buchan spent many hours trying to make them understand he was peaceful and his sudden appearance was a mistake. But communications were grossly inadequate; the Beothuk mistrust was evident, as their chief kept challenging his wisdom by continuously pointing to the armed marines and their dozens of savage, barking dogs.

In an attempt to allay their fears, Buchan gave them the few gifts he was carrying as well as much of their own equipment. Realizing the chief was still unconvinced and unsatisfied with his meager presents, he had the chief accompany him back to the depot to get the appropriate presents. To show his good faith, he left two unarmed marines behind as hostages until their chief safely returned.

Arriving at the depot, the chief was shocked to see such a large well-established site with so many more soldiers and was sure Buchan had tricked him, having returned to get more warriors, and had invited him only to disorganize his tribe.

Buchan did not perceive the chief as his hostage and allowed him to wander as desired, and during the night, he escaped to warn his people.

Meanwhile, back at the campsite, the Beothuks were cautiously pleased with the unusual display of friendship and treated their two marine guests well, who preferred to play with the curious children, including Shawnadithit, who was fascinated by the two red-haired young soldiers. Red meant they somehow possessed the tribe's attributes. The tribe felt relations were finally starting to improve.

Returning to his campsite in a terror, the chief called his bewildered tribe together in a circle and hastily explained how they had been betrayed, that there were numerous white men with guns and dogs preparing to swoop down and annihilate them once and for all. Some were shocked, a few indifferent, but most, including Shawnadithit, simply did not believe their chief, who was a known troublemaker and a warmonger. The elders demanded a war council and a vote, noting the armed marines already had ample opportunity to kill them in a surprise attack, as had been their tactic in the past.

The chief, prancing and shouting, incensed at their disrespect for him, demanded the two unarmed marines be put to death immediately then to promptly separate into bands, break camp, and proceed at once into the dense forest. The elders refused to consent, pointing out it was the Beothuk tradition not to hurt any unarmed man who came to them seeking peace, insisting the marines be released first. The chief argued the marines would know the direction they had fled and Buchan with his fast dog teams would catch them. In that case, the majority opted to take the marines with them, but the angry chief warned the result would be the same; Buchan would search for his men. The council pointed out that killing them would bring even greater retribution.

In spite of all the chief's theatrics and convoluted arguments, the tribe disagreed strenuously; the marines were not be killed. It was a good opportunity to break the vicious killing cycle in which they were always the loser. As the disagreement dragged on, the chief became even more infuriated, accusing his braves of wasting valuable time because they were cowards. Even though this was the greatest insult to a Beothuk and warranted a fight-to-the-death challenge to save face, they still refused to consent, realizing it was only a pressure tactic.

Finally, the chief had an insidious idea. The only way to convince the council was to deliberately lie, a cardinal crime if detected. He calmly announced that he saw thunder (cannons) in the white man's depot. This shocked the elders. They could not conceive of any possible reason to bring thunder to their campsite except for mass killing. Sorely disappointed, they reluctantly agreed with the chief's demands.

The two marines were sneakily led out of the wigwam by the chief. Once outside, other braves shot them from behind with several arrows. The elders of the tribe were appalled at such a cowardly execution. The chief then hacked their heads off and waved them in victory parade. Within a few hours, the whole tribe was heading into the dense forest in desperation, taking the severed heads with them.

Shawnadithit found the chief's action repulsive and unforgivable. The marines were kind, did nothing wrong, even gave them presents. She loved the large jaw-breaking peppermint candies and chocolate bars. Besides, the two white marines were good-looking and young. She understood why the white man hated her people so much.

Buchan, loaded with presents, returned to the gruesome sight of the naked bodies of his two decapitated young marines and the camp deserted. But he did pursue the Beothuk to take revenge; he felt they had been so victimized over the years such action should have been anticipated. He blamed himself as much as those who had gone before.

When Shawnadithit reached thirteen, her attention turned to the braves of the tribe. Nonosbawsut, four years older, was big, handsome, and especially courageous, even foolhardy. When only twelve, he had been away for two weeks on his four-day vision quest to acquire his guardian spirit. The elders believed he had been killed and gave him a funeral service. But to their astonishment, late one night, he returned with a bear's paw hung around his neck as his protector and the bear carcass on his back.

He had already single-handedly raided many fur traders' traps and salmon weirs and led several expeditions on long journeys downriver to the ocean in winter to steal the fisherman equipment, especially metal tools that had been left behind after their fully loaded fish ships departed for the winter. This was a big gamble since as of late, armed soldiers were remaining behind to guard the more valuable property.

Nonosbawsut was unique; he was the only known Beothuk to have a beard, and it was red and bushy. (This led Buchan to believe until he died the Beothuks were Viking descendants.) Nonosbawsut was also unusually intelligent and clever and particularity proud of his skill in wrecking weirs, dams, and fishing nets that blocked salmon and other fish from going upriver to spawn. To him, they were stealing his livelihood, an insidious attempt to starve his people—an act of war.

He was skillful at tracking and spying, knew the most intimate details of how the furriers operated their traplines, and had often pilfered both the animals and their traps. But such daring activities were also a display of courage to demonstrate his ability to gain favor at the next council election for chief. Shawnadithit wanted such a courageous person, but not him. She still sadly recalled the two red-haired marines who had been so kind to her and wondered if they were the good-spirit persons of her dream. She felt Nonosbawsut could better use his talents for peace. Fortunately, all the other young girls did want him, and competition was fierce.

Most of the metal tools possessed by the now remaining sixty members of the Beothuks had also come through Nonosbawsut's exploits or through his leadership. He had stolen knives, axes, fishhooks, fish lines, fishnets, canvas, and nails from the foreign fisherman, but what he cherished most, a flat-bottomed wooden rowboat (dory), still eluded him. It would also allow him to safely venture further out into the ocean to harpoon whales and harbor seals; birch bark canoes were too small and fragile for such rough waters. In addition, it would be ideal for the shallower part of the lakes and rivers. He considered it a valuable asset to his starving people, and such a chief prize would also most certainly get him elected chief.

In wintertime, the cluster of mamateeks was always a beehive of activity. After warriors, craftsmen were the most respected. They selected and cured trees to carve bows, make arrows, and fashion flint arrowheads. They made various types of spears for fighting as well as for hunting and fishing. Other skillful artisans collected the suitable birch bark and built canoes, while others constructed sleds. It was communal living; all the tribe shared the work as well as the harvest.

The women tended the fires, prepared and cooked meals, tanned and cured animal hides and made clothing, and carved birch-bark containers for food and water. Most important of all, they were the sentinels for their campsites. In such cases, they would often be captured, allowing the men to get away, as women were less likely to be killed; however, only slightly.

At sixteen, Shawnadithit, had "shiny jet-black hair, dark, vigilant, piercing eyes, which were remarkably striking and beautiful. Her teeth were white, even, and perfectly sound. Her hands and feet, small and well formed. Her manners were easy and graceful and her temper calm." She was known as the tribe's flirt, had a steady lover, but had no intention to marry. Marriage meant a dead husband before thirty with kids to raise alone.

Nonosbawsut spent his time away raiding or in council with the elders. Survival of his people and the destruction of his enemies were his priority, not women; they were a distraction from his goals. Yet he wanted a female companion, a true spirit with whom to bond. He felt Shawnadithit was pretty, outgoing, and very artistic; he liked her, but it was rumored she believed in the joining of spirits with the white devils, and that repulsed him. Besides, she still flirted with everybody.

Several girls were hardworking but not courageous. Demasduit was his age, brave, mature, and the daughter of the existing chief, but she was too independent and paid attention to nobody.

Inspired by his superior abilities, early in 1816, the tribe elected Nonosbawsut their new chief. The council offered him the peace pipe and hinted it was now time to parley with their enemies as they were superior. He adamantly refused the peace pipe, angrily lecturing his elders that he wanted the Beothuks to be masters in their own land, not half-white servants. He vowed to die free, reminding them that their sacred homeland was chosen for them by *the Voice* who created them and sent them to earth using an arrow, with instructions to live free and independent or die in that land. Nobody present dared refute the tribe's traditional wisdom.

Now respected, he asked Demasduit, now twenty, to marry him. She readily agreed, much to Shawnadithit's disappointment, who thought her sister, Easter Eve, was a perfect match for him. The council was happy to perform any ceremony for the dwindling tribe. A wedding was one of their major festive occasions in which food was consumed unsparingly, and everyone participated willingly. It was a rare happy time. There were no musical instruments, alcohol, or mind-altering drugs, but the storytelling, joking, dancing, recitation of heroic events, singing of tragic songs, and various games continued unabated for twenty-four hours or more. Shawnadithit was considered the best at acting and making creative silhouettes on the tepee. Nobody slept; fighting was strictly forbidden.

Then tragedy struck.

The large fire and noise generated from the festive activities attracted four French trappers, who crept into their campsite and opened fire on the four braves who were standing outside around the campfire flirting with Shawnadithit, who was the designated sentinel. She was shot in the leg but once again managed to escape in the ensuing chaos. The braves were not as lucky; all four were shot dead.

Cut off from their food supply, life for the Beothuks was now below subsistence. More English fishermen were living along the coast year-round, constructing permanent dams and weirs and placing nets across the river. Their dogs were trained to bark to warn them every time the Beothuk approached the seashore. Organized armed militias soon appeared and pursued them ever greater distances inland, shooting them down like criminals. Their ancestral seashore now belonged to foreigners.

The French and Micmac fur trappers, who also lived year-round in cabins with their Micmac wives, were killing or trapping animals for their skins only, leaving the meat to spoil. This was desecrating the sacred spirit of the animals. Hunting was a spiritual activity and had to be carried out in the manner that was respectable for the animal. The Great Spirit allowed them to take only as much as needed for survival; to kill recklessly was evil, and as nature's caretakers, it was their responsibility to keep nature in balance.

The trappers also kept dogs for pulling their sleds, and their barking could be heard at night, scaring the animals away; at times, even attacked them. The Beothuks despised such intrusions upsetting Mother Nature's balance.

As well, noise from firearms was stampeding the herds of caribou, which in turn were destroying the Beothuk deer fences. For survival, they had no choice but to move progressively deeper up the lake into the forest where there was little food. They were relentlessly hunted, and there was no longer any safe place to hide. The only reprieve was that the Algonquin tribes no longer came to their island and raided their camps for slaves as there were only forty Beothuks remaining.

The tribe's pathetic condition forced Nonosbawsut to react. In the fall of 1818, in full daylight in a vicious snowstorm, he led a small group of braves on a daring raid to the mouth of the Exploits River and finally got his prize, capturing a flat-bottomed boat right under the nose of the chief white devil. Equally valuable was its load of fishing equipment. That winter, living was good; they used the nets to trap lake trout and the twine to snare rabbits. The tribe celebrated their new chief's success, and soon every fisherman on the coast began to hear troublesome rumors about a giant red bushy-bearded Indian who mysteriously carried out daring exploits on the coast. Many of the superstitious fishermen believed it to be an Indian ghost taking revenge for their mistreatment, and such gross exaggeration was causing mass panic.

What Nonosbawsut didn't know was that the new governor of his land, Sir Charles Hamilton, was responding to the fishermen's concerns and had authorized an armed attempt to recover the stolen property. With the legal writ, in the spring of 1819, John Peyton Jr., his father, and two other businessmen had hired eight handpicked heavily armed men and had journeyed up the Exploits River to Red Indian Lake in search of the "red savages," and on March 1 had found the main Beothuk campsite near the lakeshore and was already hiding outside awaiting an opportune time to attack.

From his hideaway, John Peyton Jr. could see the sail canvas from his boat was being used as covering for the chief's mamateek. His salmon boat and nets could not be far away. However, he did not want to kill anyone as the government was offering a £100 reward for the safe capture and return of a Red Indian slave to act as a goodwill ambassador.

Inside, Nonosbawsut's attention was not of war. He stared in awe at his newborn son. After years of marriage, he had finally produced an heir. The Great Spirit was shining on his people at last. He envisioned a future legendary chief, one that would destroy his enemies and liberate his oppressed people. Outside it was cold and stormy, but nobody noticed; the ritual birth celebrations continued all night with dancing and song, cumulating with the ceremonial anointing of the boy's body in red ochre at daylight and bequeathing him with his own regal name. Then, tired, all fell into a deep sleep.

By morning, the snowstorm had abated; it dawned bright and frigid. John Peyton Jr. seized the opportunity and ambushed the camp from the forested side. The terrified tribe scattered in horror from the attackers to find the only escape route available was out onto the open lake, Shawnadithit and Demasduit among them.

Demasduit, weak from childbirth, easily became bogged down in the deep freshly fallen snow and was easily apprehended. In the -30ºC bone-chilling wind, on her knees on the frozen lake, she opened her coat and exposed her bare breasts to show John Peyton Jr.'s vigilantes she was a new nursing mother, begging for mercy. Through her sobs, she desperately tried to make them understand her predicament, pointing to her belly to indicate she just had a new baby, but they laughed and mocked her, believing she was offering them sex.

Nonosbawsut, observing his wife being surrounded and taunted, was furious and decided to confront them to rescue her, knowing he would be shot, but without her, his son would die. He handed Shawnadithit his son and asked her to raise him in his absence then instructed his tribe to circle back and hide into the safety of the nearby woods while he drew their attention and to monitor the outcome. If he failed, to flee inland into the denser forest.

John Peyton Jr. tied Demasduit's hands behind her back with his handkerchief, planning on holding her as hostage—a negotiating tool until his property was returned. Nonosbawsut broke a small branch from a tree and placed it on his forehead as a symbol of peace and walked slowly toward them. Reaching them, he bowed, opened his arms to show he was hiding no weapons, and made peace gestures to John Peyton Jr., indicating his wife's condition. John Peyton Jr. responded callously by drawing pictures of his boat and property into the snow and pointing to Demasduit as a trade. Nonosbawsut pointed to the boat, which was hidden away in the forest many miles up the lake. But then, John Peyton Jr.'s father, the butcher, saw an opportunity to capture him as well and ordered the men to seize him. Nonosbawsut could see his fragile wife, who was also suffering from consumption, was deteriorating fast in the frigid weather, lifted her up, and began to untie the handkerchief. Six men surrounded him. Nonosbawsut felled the first man who approached him with a single blow. The other swarmed him only to have another man rendered unconscious with a second blow. A ferocious fistfight ensued, and for a time, he single-handedly held off all eight attackers. Seeing Nonosbawsut so outnumbered, his brother and another brave quickly emerged from the trees and joined the fray.

Nonosbawsut then spied John Peyton Sr. among the command group that was watching—the butcher who was responsible for the massacre of dozens of his extended family. Infuriated, he viciously grabbed him by the throat and squeezed with all the strength and hate his 230-pound frame could muster. Several men punched and kicked him mercilessly, trying to break his grasp, to no avail. John Peyton Sr., now over seventy, collapsed to the ground with Nonosbawsut on top with his knee firmly embedded into his chest, suffocating him.

John Peyton Jr. hesitated shooting, knowing it was now illegal to kill Indians, but as precious seconds ticked away, he could see his aged father was now near death from strangulation, and his eight men were no match in fistfighting with the three Beothuks. He directed his men to shoot only Nonosbawsut. Two bullets pierced his body. But he continued to squeeze.

Astounded he did not collapse and wary of hitting his father, John Peyton Jr. ordered two men to stab him repeatedly from behind with bayonets, but still Nonosbawsut refused to release his death grip. Now terrified, fearing Nonosbawsut was the supernatural Indian spirit of the local legend, several others tried to crush his head with their gun butts, while others stabbed him relentlessly from both sides. Finally he collapsed, chopped to bits like a butchered caribou, a gruesome sight that sickened some of the men.

Recovering, John Peyton Sr., in a fit of rage, ordered the men to shoot the other two Beothuks as revenge, who, without weapons, had already begun racing back toward the trees when the shooting began. Both were shot in the back.

As Demasduit was dragged away screaming and struggling, she knew that horrific sight of her brave, devoted husband with his two faithful braves lying dead, staining the clean white snow a bright red on the tranquil lake in the morning sunshine, would be her last memories of her people. For her, there could be no return. Even worse, she had only nursed her newborn son twice. She wondered if by some miracle of the Great Spirit, Shawnadithit could somehow save him.

John Peyton Jr. was now terrified as well; he had a serious dilemma on his hands. As the designated magistrate for the area, it was his official expedition; the writ had been issued in his name, limiting his authority to reclaiming his property, with specific instructions to commit no harm. He had been privy to the colonial government Red Indian Act enactment, which authorized the same penalty as for killing Europeans; thus he had committed murder. He had no idea what to do with Demasduit. But his father did; she was a £100 commodity to be sold.

Believing the Englishmen were on an Indian hunt, the remainder of the tribe headed deep into the forest, leaving Demasduit behind. John Peyton Jr. could not execute her in front of his Christian men; that would undoubtedly warrant a conviction of murder, unlike in Nonosbawsut's case, where his men could testify it was self-defense. Besides, killing a defenseless woman would be a moral issue in which his private vigilantes, who were all family men, would not want to become embroiled. He had no choice but to take her home with him. And he had not even reclaimed any of his property.

In the John Peyton Jr. household, Demasduit soon discovered the butcher, John Peyton Sr., was her captor's father. She was now terrified as well as suffering from malnutrition and consumption.

Not wanting a sick, stinky savage contaminating his respectable home, John Peyton Jr. gave her to the Rev. John Leigh, a Church of England priest, as a house servant. But even there, she was inferior. Being a heathen, in order to live on God's property, even as a servant, to make her presence more palatable she first had to be rechristened Mary March, after Jesus's mother and the month in which she was kidnapped.

In spite of the Rev. Leigh's perceived Christian charity, his actions bothered him. Not because she was a captured slave, but some of his parishioners perceived this as not only immoral and hypocritical for a man of God but also illegal. With her capture being full public knowledge, to ease his conscience, he had no alternative but to surrender her to the government authorities in St. John's and attempt to explain the unique circumstances surrounding her capture, hoping John Peyton Jr. and his men would not be indicted. The Peytons, after all, were the church's chief contributors.

By this time, entrepreneurs and amateur philanthropists like David Buchan and William Cormack were fully cognizant the uncontrolled English settlers were close to committing genocide. The fishermen and trappers openly publicized it was their aim to completely liquidate their Red Indian pests, and these good Samaritans, often using their own time and money, were working tirelessly urging the government to make a more conscientious effort to establish contacts with the Beothuks before it was too late, and to rein in the local vigilantes. It was well-known the French and Micmac trappers had absconded the Beothuk inland winter food supply, the English fishermen had cut their summer food source from the coast, and the Beothuk were being decimated by disease for which they had no immunity or for which there was no treatment. Their extinction was inevitable.

As an act of piousness, in St. John's, Demasduit was accepted into the home of the Newfoundland's governor, Sir Charles Hamilton, where his wife painted her portrait and afforded her medical attention.

Then, as a goodwill gesture and in some small way to make amends, Hamilton offered to return her. She adamantly refused, explaining she would be killed for associating with the white man, whose diseases had already killed most of her people, and they were effectively in a self-imposed quarantine. However, against her strenuous objections, during the summer of 1819, the government showered Demasduit with gifts and made a number of attempts to return her; all unsuccessful.

Capt. David Buchan, a genuine friend of the Beothuks, insisted on transferring Demasduit from St. John's to Botwood in his fishing schooner, such that after the season ended and the ground became frozen in November to make transportation easier, he would personally make the arduous journey overland to Red Indian Lake with her, having already accepted—and spent—the funds from the compassionate peoples of St. John's and Notre Dame Bay had donated for her return. He wanted to make peace with the Beothuks, help them with their food shortage and disease problems, and of course, explain why Demasduit was forced to return.

Buchan also wanted to obtain firsthand assessment of the true plight of the Beothuks and their numbers. Until then, he provided Demasduit with a warm comfortable cabin on his vessel, the *Grasshopper*, at Botwood. But by November, she was suffering acutely from consumption, too weak to travel. He had his personal doctor care for her daily, but there was no cure for tuberculosis. Despite his gallant efforts, she died on January 8, 1820.

To fulfill his promise to take her home, Buchan placed her body in a coffin and took her overland to her campsite on the lake where she had been captured, but the site was deserted. He placed her coffin in a crudely built animal-proof shelter, performed a Christian burial service, and departed.

Shawnadithit had indeed admirably adopted her friend's baby, but the tribe had only thirty-one members remaining; none were nurturing mothers. The infant died of starvation a few days later and was given a ceremonial funeral along with his father and placed together in the spirit house. The following spring, her tribe found Demasduit's coffin, returned her to her village, and placed her beside them.

For Shanawadihit, life continued to deteriorate. Her closest friend and lover froze to death in the winter of 1822 on a raiding party to the coast for food. Most of the remaining people were now females, the young, or the sick, all suffering from starvation. Her father and uncle were now the two most able braves in the tribe.

In the summer, unable to find food in the wilderness, in desperation, her uncle Longnon and his daughter decided run the gauntlet of unfriendly English fisherman and trappers along the Exploits River and attempt to reach Badger Bay junction to collect mussels and other shellfish to bring back to the sick. They travelled only at night.

Shawnadithit, after a week of living on magpies, herbs, and berries, became nervous when her uncle failed to returned. With her mother and sister, she left their campsite to search for them. After another week of travelling, they found them rotting and partly eaten by animals on the beach at Badger Bay, shot by the local fishermen.

It got worse.

By the spring of 1823, the few remaining Beothuks were barely alive, acutely suffering from malnutrition and disease, almost too weak to move. Shawnadithit's mother and sister were seriously ill from consumption. Without food, her father gallantly led them down the Exploits for mussels, which was always available in shallow water on the coast after the ice moved offshore.

Near the seashore, they were walking single file on thin slob ice to reach a reef when they were suddenly fired upon by local fishermen from behind the trees. In making their escape, Shawnadithit's father fell through the ice and remained in the frigid water feigning drowning until his family escaped and the fishermen left. By then, he was almost comatose, managing only to drag himself out after a long titanic struggle. Luckily, the family rendezvoused with him several hours later, but by now, he was barely alive. Lighting a fire was impossible; it would attract the gunmen. They just wrapped him in a fur blanket. He died of exposure during the night.

Unable to feed themselves, Shawnadithit convinced her mother and sister that she knew where a white trapper lived near the river, who had seen her many times stealing salmon from his weir and just smiled and waved. He might be her good spirit. They adamantly disagreed. But starving, a few days later, they acquiesced and sought his help.

She was partly correct. The trapper, William Cull, took them to his home, fed them, and cared for them for a few days until they were well enough to travel. But by law, he was now forced to surrender Red

Indians to the authorities in the area, who happened to be represented locally by John Peyton Jr.

For the official register, John Peyton Jr. gave them Christian names. Shawnadithit he renamed Nancy April, since that was the month she was captured; her sister he called Easter Eve as it was also the day before Easter. Her mother, Doodebewshet, was referred to simply as the Mother, as they figured she would die soon die of consumption.

For months, they lived at the Peyton's home as guests and were treated well. Shawnadithit, who was relatively healthy, liked the warm stove-heated room in the well-built house with comfortable beds. But much to their displeasure, they were all given a bath by the servants, who removed the ingrained red ochre—which took several hours—and gave them new white man's clothes. Shawnadithit especially liked the dry rubber boots, which she wore over her skin boots. The only detriment was that *the butcher* lived with him, and they were all terrified of him.

Nonetheless, Shawnadithit showed her appreciation by willingly doing the family chores, but her mother and sister, in spite of trying hard to lend a hand, were very weak and tired, suffering long bouts of hacking, choking cough with discharges of blood and mucus, sometimes too sick to move. It was obvious to all they were critically ill.

Opposition to the slaughter of the Red Indians was slowly, however grudgingly, increasing. Many European families were living year-round along the coast of Notre Dame Bay, and government authorities were warning not to harm the Red Indians except in self-defense. A few were sympathetic, most were indifferent, but all knew the tribe was dying. Some made long journeys by boat to get a firsthand view of the savage Red Indian family. To their astonishment, they were not red but radiated a fair, pale complexion without any acne or blemishes, unlike most like them. They were tall, slim, and walked perfectly erect without hunched shoulders, had perfect teeth, shiny long black hair, sparkling ebony eyes, and were very civilized. Not only the men, but also the women, saw them as beautiful. It was the opposite of what they were led to believe. If it were not for their dreaded cough demon, they would be perfect.

As a goodwill gesture, a collection was made for them. The authorities gave Shawnadithit and her relatives a small rowboat, loaded it with food, clothes, and gifts for their people as enticement to act as emissaries of peace for their tribe, and left them conveniently at the mouth the Exploits River.

Shawnadithit was now caught between two worlds. She knew her people would make a ritual sacrifice of any tribal member who voluntarily made contact with the Europeans as redemption for those they had killed. Even worse, the removal of red ochre meant a rejection by the tribe, a punishment reserved for criminals, and severe restitutions were mandatory before reinstatement. But that was now academic; she believed the last ten members of her people were by now all dead from disease and starvation. If not, they knew of her sacred dream, and this would verify it.

It didn't matter; her mother and sister were too weak to travel. All her time and energy was consumed in keeping them alive. She remained on the sandy beach where they were left. Her sister Easter Eve died within two weeks. She sewed her body in a birch-bark blanket, covered it in red ochre, then paddled upriver to a sandy point near their ancestral home on Red Indian Lake—the only place her family had ever experienced any happiness—and buried her.

Shawnadithit was heartbroken; it was clear her mother was dying too. Without eating or sleeping, she held her mother in her arms for three days and nights and chanted her people's last lament until she expired. She then performed her race's last burial ceremony and laid her next to her sister.

Hungry and grieving, next day in a blinding snowstorm, she set out on foot for the coast to search for her good-spirit person.

She knew she was the last of her race.

Several days later, Shawnadithit heard dogs barking and aimlessly followed the sound. Though scared, it was a more pleasant sound than the growl the prowling bear that circled her one night while sleeping alone under the trees. Emerging from the forest, she staggered through the deep snow toward the first house she saw on the coast, too tired and hungry to be cautious. As the dogs ran toward her, an old man appeared at the door and pointed his gun toward her.

She fell at her knees and closed her eyes, expecting the worst.

To her surprise, he recalled the dogs, placed his gun against the porch, and hobbled to greet her. She pointed to her mouth. He gently helped her to her feet and led her into his house. It was warm, and the smell of freshly cooked stew filled her nostrils. She was eternally grateful as the old lady smiled and fetched her bowl of thick rabbit stew, which she ravenously consumed with her fingers or by slurping directly from the bowl. Famished, she indicated another, then another, to the enjoyment of the old man who thought she would eat him out of house and home. Finished at last, she indicated to sleep on the floor. The old woman led her upstairs to the spare bedroom. Without removing her sealskin boots or her fully clad caribou-skin attire, she flopped unto the bed and was instantly asleep.

After sleeping for ten hours, Shawnadithit awoke to see a delicious breakfast prepared for her. Her rescuers did not appear to be scared of her, and she felt safe and relaxed with them. They seemed always cheerful and contented.

Finding the house warm and stuffy, during the next week, she worked outside, insisting at helping the old man at even his most laborious chores. She could see he was intrigued by her fierce independence but was treating her as if she were his own daughter, and she quickly formed a bond with him. Being old, they certainly needed someone to care for them, and they appeared to be the good spirits of her dream. She smiled in return, happy she had found a home so fast. She thanked the Great Spirit.

However, Shawnadithit's hopes were soon dashed when they returned from fishing one day to see the house filled with armed men arguing with the old woman. Her heart sank. A man in uniform showed her his badge and indicated for her to follow. She guessed she would be taken to the forest and shot and clung to the old man crying and pleading for help. He angrily ordered the men with guns outside. They obeyed. After consoling her and giving her a big hamper of food, some clothes, and a bear hug from both the old man and the teary-eyed old woman, she understood they had no authority to retain her.

After a long motorboat ride in calm water among the beautiful islands her people knew so well, she was taken to a place she had been before, Exploits Island, back to the home of John Peyton Jr. She was not really disappointed to learn that she would live as his servant as he had been fair and honest with her and her family before; they lived in a warm, comfortable large home, and he was the chief (magistrate) who could keep her safe from the renegade fishermen. However, having to live in the same house with his father, the butcher, repulsed her.

John Peyton Jr. and his father were soon to find Shawnadithit was "mild mannered, courteous, pleasant, and very intelligent." They could see she had accepted her fate as a servant and was trying to learn English. Like Demasduit before her, she was very proud of her heritage but would easily take offense if she thought she had been insulted. She proved to be more disciplined and rational than his three white servant counterparts in every respect. The Old Man, as John Peyton Sr. was known to his family, liked Shawnadithit and requested her as his own private servant, and inexplicably, treated her with great respect. She soon became the fascination of the local people, even attracting interest in the colonial government.

Shawnadithit found it ironical that fate led her to live under the same roof as the butcher and they needed each other's help. She wondered if he felt any remorse for slaughtering so many of her people. His utmost kindness was puzzling to her; she was just another savage. More surprising was that the trapper William Cull was his employee, as Cull did no harm to her people at any time.

As time passed and Shawnadithit began to communicate in broken English and motions, she learned the story of John Peyton Jr.'s life and realized he was the unfortunate victim of the location he chose when he first came to her land. It lay along the main migration routes of the Beothuks, and by that time, a full-scale war was already raging with the foreigners. His engagement in inshore cod fishing with his own schooner affected them only slightly, and Shawnadithit understood he too had to make a living, but the extreme greed of maintaining twelve salmon fishing stations to completely block the first thirty miles of their river and to shoot all of the seals, animals, and wild fowl they found was reprehensible and devastating to the environment as well as to her people—an insane concept that was both puzzling and foreign to her. She found them intelligent enough to know that fur trapping along the Exploits River and around Red Indian Lake would adversely impact their livelihood. The white man seemed to want to kill and destroy everything, not just the Beothuks.

She found the drunken parties at the Peyton house as obnoxious as any war council in her tribe, with a lot more fighting, but they all appeared scared of her, even when drunk. The smoke from the men's pipes and cigarettes caused her to cough, and to her dismay, they smoked all the time. Some even chewed tobacco and spat it on the ground. To her they were the *savages.*

Shawnadithit was fascinated by the rituals of the Anglican Church and their belief in just one God and attended whenever possible. She too had a supreme Good Spirit. Because of her low status, she was relegated to the back row where it was oft times difficult to see the preacher's actions, but she was thankful.

She loved clothes, and weddings were her favorite festival, with the bride's puffy white gowns. These feasts often found her jumping, dancing, and laughing. However, even an invitation to dance by a man would make her angry. No man was permitted to touch her body in any way. Beothuk culture allowed only one man, and hers was dead.

Funerals were more interesting and complex; she did not like them. They were reminders of her lost people. She realized white people were not so different; they believed in the afterlife, as she did, but why they left no war tools or food in the burial sites for the journey of the loved ones to the other side confused her. Did they starve their dead too?

But it was John Peyton Jr.'s children that touched Shawnadithit's heart. Without a family or a child of her own, she doted on them—much to the frustration of their parents—and was pleased they accepted her as their mom. His son, Thomas, adored her. (Thomas Peyton went on to become a justice of the peace, a magistrate, and a member of the Newfoundland Legislature for Newfoundland North in St. John's.)

One day, Shawnadithit was pleasantly surprised to see Lt. Buchan appear at the Peyton household with a load of gifts for her. He had a multitude of questions about her race and how to help them, even offering to return her to them. As before, she refused, saying they were all dead.

During the next few months, she spent a great deal of time with Buchan and came to trust him, answering his many questions and those of his newspaper reporter friends. Buchan heard through her broken English what happened to his two marines and many of the horrific tragedies that had befallen her people. He offered to take her to England to live with him as a guest, study English at college to record the history of her people, meet King George IV, and tour Europe as a celebrity Red Indian princess. Again she refused. John Peyton Jr. treated her kinder than he did his own wife, bought her nice clothes and gifts when away; she owed him a debt of service. Besides, she still recalled the tragic story of her aunt Oubee. The dream of being a Beothuk princess died with her people, and very few white men considered her any more than a savage beast.

After five years as a servant at the Peyton household, one day, Buchan arrived with a smiling gentleman called William Cormack who explained he was president of a foundation to save the Beothuks. She found that insulting; now that the white man had murdered all her race, they were pretending to save them. In her broken English, she angrily assailed him on his stupidity and arrogance. But he did not get upset. Instead, he bowed and apologized, offering to take her to St. John's to reside with him in his large home as an honored guest; and this time, *she* would have a servant and an English teacher. Her only requirement was to limn chronicles of her people and her homeland for him and to record the language of her people.

Shawnadithit couldn't believe her good fortune. Drawing was her lifelong dream; she readily agreed.

At last, Shawnadithit had found her good spirit in Cormack. She began to read and speak English. He supplied her with an overabundance of materials for drawing, an art she so loved. In her own language, she wrote down 325 of their most common words, twenty-one numerals, and the months of the year. For a few months, she churned out the history of her people, happily spending long days drawing detailed maps of her home on Red Indian Lake (which later proved to be remarkably accurate). Her sketches not only included still life objects like canoes, clothing, animals, wigwams, bows, and arrows, or of her people, but also accurate depictions of white man's raiding expeditions and their confrontations, including the Peyton massacre in which Demasduit was captured and her husband, Nonosbawsut, murdered, even the decapitation of the Buchan's marines and how they danced around the severed heads displayed on pikes at a feast in their new campsite. She enjoyed drawing pictures of their great harvest feasts, competitive games, festivities, even burial rituals. She planned on writing down all she knew for the man she trusted implicitly.

Cormack was both ecstatic and impressed by her dedication and honesty; she related the real story, even to the detriment of her own race. He figured a book could be published within a few years. (Almost everything we now know about the Beothuks came from her.)

But her Great Spirit was unkind to her; that too was short-lived. The cough demon was viciously attacking her body; she was often lethargic, unable to leave her bed due to barking cough. A renowned Scottish surgeon, Dr. William Carson, Newfoundland's surgeon general, attended to her personally. (Sir William Carson would later become speaker of the house in Newfoundland's House of Assembly)

Then worse news.

In the fall, Cormack was recalled to England, and she was transferred to live in the house of his friend, Newfoundland's attorney general, James Simms, for security until he returned. It broke her heart to see her most trusted friend leave. She responded to his kindness by giving him a lock of her hair and two keepsake stones from her home on Red Indian Lake, her most treasured worldly possessions, tiny microcosms of the great territory in which the Beothuk once ruled supreme. Such a rare gift could only be presented by a chief or his princess in recognition of a *good-spirit* person.

She lived with James Simms or in the St. John's hospital for the next nine months but never left her bed. She would not see her good spirit again. Her own spirit was fading. She died on June 6, 1829, at twenty-nine, of tuberculosis, the cough demon, just days before he returned.

And her race died with her.

A postmortem examination on her found that her skull exhibited a certain uniqueness, and almost as if in sadistic revenge, her head was removed from her body and sent to London's Royal College of Physicians and then in 1938 transferred to the Royal College of Surgeons for more extensive analysis. The rest of her remains were buried in the cemetery of St. Mary the Virgin Church on the south side of St. John's.

As if to completely expunge Shawnadithit and her people's memory from existence, in 1903, the graveyard was dismantled to make way for a railroad right-of-way. Then as a final desecration, her skull and medical records were destroyed during the German blitz on London.

Only a simple monument of her existence today remains. It reads in part, "This spot is the burying place of Nancy Shawnadithit, the last of the Beothuks, who died on June 6, 1829."

Modern archeologists have discovered hundreds of Beothuk campsites and burial grounds scattered in every nook and cranny of Newfoundland, including Boyd's Cove, where Shawnadithit possibly lived during her summers on the coast. To most, they are popular tourist attractions, but to many, they are ghostly mute testaments of mankind's greatest inhumanity to man.

The Peytons were never charged for any of their Red Indian slaughters. At the grand jury inquiry, the judge, after hearing all twelve testimonies of the men involved, noted that their ridiculous contradictions were undoubtedly "a concoction" but, without opposing witnesses, had no choice but to conclude, "No malice on the part of Peyton's party, as kidnapping a Beothuk was offered 100 pounds to act as a bridge to her people."

Magistrate John Bland during his controversial investigation into rumors of "Red Indians shot down like deer" for target practice concluded the Beothuks were indeed being massacred like animals and recorded in his summation, "The British like the Spanish before them will have affixed to their character the indelible reproach of having extirpated a whole race of people."

His report was considered tantamount to treason by the British government and summarily archived.

Sedition or not, time would prove his ominous, prophetic insight troublingly accurate.

Ironically, history would verify Shawnadithit's shaman's prediction; she would become the most notable of her people, but in his wildest dreams, or hallucinations, he could never have predicted the reason: the last person of genocide.

In 1999, *The Telegram* newspaper online invited readers to vote for the most notable aboriginal person of the past one thousand years. Shawnadithit captured 57 percent of the total votes.

Shawnadithit's dream of being a famous princess also came true. Just twenty-two years after her death, in 1851, the newspaper *The Newfoundlander* had proclaimed her *The Princess of Terra Nova.*

Much has been penned to explain away our direct implication in the extinction of the Beothuks. But if we were as internally honest as our outward piety and flattering words indicate, we'd face the truth and admit our attitude toward First Nations peoples have changed little. Only when we can accept that all mankind is equal and of one family can we begin to resolve our prejudices.

Edwards Brothers, Inc.
Thorofare, NJ USA
May 20, 2011